Kissing the Lizard

Biography

JUSTIN DAVID is a child of Wolverhampton who has lived and worked in East London for most of his adult life. He graduated from the MA Creative and Life Writing at Goldsmiths, University of London and is a founder member of Leather Lane Writers. His writing has appeared in many print and online anthologies and his debut novella, *The Pharmacist*, was published by Salt as part of their Modern Dreams series. It was described in the Times Literary Supplement as '*the perfect introduction to a singular voice in gay literature.*' *Kissing the Lizard* is a prequel to *The Pharmacist*.

He is also a well-known photographer. His images of artists, writers, performers and muscians have appeared on the pages of numerous newspapers and magazines including: The Times, The Guardian, Attitude, Beige, Classical Music Magazine, Gay Times, Out There, Pink Paper, QX and Time Out.

Justin is one half of Inkandescent with Nathan Evans. Their first offering, *Threads*, featuring Nathan's poetry and Justin's photography, was long-listed for the Polari First Book Prize. It was supported using public funding by Arts Council England. In 2021, amidst the Covid-19 pandemic, they published their first collection, ~~MAIN~~STREAM: *An Anthology of Stories from the Edges,* championing underrepresented voices.

Praise for Justin David and
Kissing the Lizard

'This beautifully creepy novella manages to be both macabre and terrifying, yet also shot through with a humour that is blacker than black. I loved it and devoured it in one sitting.'
SJ WATSON, author of *Before I Go to Sleep*

'There's not much rarer than a working class voice in fiction, except maybe a gay working class voice.
We need writers like Justin David.'
PAUL McVEIGH, author of *The Good Son*

Praise for Justin David and
The Pharmacist

'As lubricious as early Alan Hollinghurst, *The Pharmacist*
is a welcome reissue from Inkandescent, and the perfect
introduction to a singular voice in gay literature.'
JUDE COOK, THE TIMES LITERARY SUPPLEMENT

'*The Pharmacist* is a rare thing of perfection: a contemporary
novella that reads like both a European classic and a page-
turner. The writing is superb. Sense of place, story, insight into
the human condition, gave me everything that I wanted from
a work of fiction. Not five stars but an entire galaxy!'
VG LEE, author of *Mr Oliver's Object of Desire*

'At the heart of David's *The Pharmacist* is an oddly touching
and bizarre love story, a modern day Harold and Maude set in
the drugged-up world of pre-gentrification Shoreditch. The
dialogue, especially, bristles with glorious life.'
JONATHAN KEMP, author of *London Triptych*

'A drug-fuelled, drug-fucked, sweat and semen-drenched
exploration of love and loss in the deathly hallows of twenty-
first century London. Justin David's prose is as sharp as a
hypodermic needle. Unflinching, uncomfortable but always
compelling, *The Pharmacist* finds the true meaning of love in
the most unlikely places.'
NEIL McKENNA, author of *Fanny and Stella*

'Sexy, wistful, wise, haunting and totally full of surprises.
A real ride.'
NINA WADIA

Kissing the Lizard

Justin David

Inkandescent
by outsiders for outsiders

Inkandescent

First published by Inkandescent, 2020
This edition published by Inkandescent, 2022
Text Copyright © 2022 Justin David
Cover Design Copyright © 2022 Joe Mateo

Publisher's note: a version of *Kissing the Lizard* was included in
He's Done Ever So Well for Himself by Justin David,
published by Inkandescent in 2018

A CIP catalogue record for this book
is available from the British Library

Printed in the UK by Severn, Gloucester

MIX
Paper from
responsible sources
FSC® C022174

ISBN 978-1-912620-21-0 (paperback)
ISBN 978-1-912620-18-0 (ebook)

1 3 5 7 9 10 8 6 4 2

www.inkandescent.co.uk

For my bestie, Joe Mateo

25 years. Happy Anniversary, you gorgeous man.

"Will you walk into my parlour?" said the spider to the fly;
"'Tis the prettiest little parlour that ever you did spy.
The way into my parlour is up a winding stair,
And I have many pretty things to show when you are there."

The Spider and the Fly
MARY HOWITT 1799 – 1888

Old Compton Street is simmering. Jamie registers the summer joy outside the coffee shop and rests his chin on a hand with listless resignation. Everyone has gone wild at the first sign of moderate sunlight. T-shirts are wrenched from milky torsos, men kiss in the street, shirtless bikers ride roughshod through Soho. Everyone's leaving work early to grab what they can of the rays. Businessmen drink beer in the street, abandoning ties, collars undone at the neck. Jamie can't join in. He's cut off. Three years an art student, in the capital, and no closer to being part of it.

The broken air conditioning in The Crêperie has resulted in a thick haze of steam and smoke.

'Do you think we'll ever see America?' Billy asks, looking up from a book. He draws deeply on a Marlboro—a duty-free gift from when Jamie's mum and dad spent a package holiday in Magaluf. He exhales into the already choked room.

'I don't know,' Jamie says, waving away smoke. 'I'm not convinced I'll ever get back to London, let alone reach the States.'

'Well you're here now, aren't you?'

'For one more night but then I have to go back to that wretched place,' Jamie says, rolling up the sleeves of his paisley shirt and unbuttoning his waistcoat.

Billy places the fag in his mouth and leafs through the other books Jamie has piled up on the table, next to a ball of loose red wool and his length of knitting impaled on size eight needles. A volume about alien abductions by Whitley Strieber provokes a curl from Billy's lip. Another one—*Feel the Fear and Do It*

Anyway—incites a cartoon scowl. He holds up a third book and frowns. '*The Prophetic Insights,*' he says. 'Really?'

'I'm searching.'

'What for? The knit-your-own-aura-brigade?'

Jamie returns to the accommodation pages of *Time Out*. 'Nothing under seventy-five pounds a week.'

'Well if you hadn't run back to Mummy and Daddy so quickly…'

'I didn't have any money, Billy.'

Billy stares at Jamie's hair. 'You could save ten pounds a month if you stopped bleaching that mop.'

A clique of art students Jamie recognises from St. Martin's cackle over cappuccinos near the window. Plates clatter. A radio crackles, losing and regaining its signal—issuing a broken chorus of *Tubthumping* by Chumbawumba. The coffee shop is full of French and Germans and Turks and Americans. Everyone else seems to be having a great time.

'If you'd taken that job with the magazine you'd be on an all-expenses paid trip to India by now.'

Jamie throws the *Time Out* across the table. Billy, still within the cosy confines of his final year, hasn't yet felt freedom slipping away.

'Free holidays don't pay the rent,' Jamie says. 'If I could afford to work for nothing, I'd have a huge portfolio and a contract at *The Guardian*—not living back with my parents in the arse end of nowhere.'

A tanned rent-boy brushes past the table—an outline of an

unfinished William Morris design peeking out of a loosely buttoned shirt. Jamie watches Billy's eyes trail his studded leather belt and bubble-butt. The youth takes his window seat, from where he has solicited every weekend during Jamie's time at art school.

'Some folks know how to make money,' Billy says.

'You're meant to be with me, not eyeing up the local trade.'

Billy leans across the table and takes Jamie's hand. Jamie pulls back but Billy holds on tight. 'This is Soho. Not the West Midlands. You think anyone gives a shit if I hold your hand?' Billy squeezes even tighter. He is looking into Jamie, his gentle opalescent eyes lined with kohl. Jamie feels himself yield. 'Maybe you should take more notice of those books you read— meditate or something.'

Hard to stay positive, Jamie thinks. 'You know, that talentless bitch, Saffron Delany—'

'Still gnawing away at that bone?'

'She left St Martin's last year and did three months at Vogue without pay. She's done pop videos, photo shoots and now she's famous for doing fuck all. Can't open a newspaper without seeing her smug face. This time next year, her father will probably *buy* her Channel Four for her birthday and she'll be married to Lance Lewes.'

Billy laughs. 'It won't last. Everyone knows he's got a touch of lavender. You'll get your chance.'

'Will I?' Jamie asks.

'*Anything* is possible,' Billy continues. 'I might win one of those photographic competitions I entered. Who knows? I could get a big contract.'

'You're deluded, Billy. It doesn't happen to people like us.'

'Oh, here comes Tess of the D'Urbervilles again.'

'When I finished my degree, I thought I'd be on my way—list of contacts, a little place to live in London. Look at me now—working a supermarket checkout. Mother's driving me mad.'

Billy nods at the books on the table. 'She'll wipe the floor with you if she catches you reading that rubbish.'

Billy's right. Gloria has a temperament neatly suited to British border control. Jamie touches the cover of *The Prophetic Insights* protectively. 'It's the key.'

Billy picks up the book and reads the blurb. '*From six-hundred hours of channelling extra-terrestrials, Prunella Small brings to us a new wisdom for the New Age. For anyone questioning an ever more confusing cosmos, The Prophetic Insights offer the reassurance and knowledge required to go beyond fear and trust the universe.*' He drops the book on the table as if having discovered a turd in his hand. 'We've got to get you out of this situation. Up there, you're not surrounded by people who can nurture you. We've got to get you back to London.'

'I'm twenty-two. There are things I should have done by now. List of clubs I should know. I want to publish a novel before I'm thirty.'

'Come on, what are you having?' Billy urges. 'We've sent the waitress away twice.'

Jamie fingers the space in his wallet where he might keep a

few notes. Empty. 'I'm not hungry.'

'I'll treat you.' Billy turns the menu to Jamie—an entirely vegetarian selection, couscous, pancakes stuffed with spinach—the sort of fare that bores him rigid.

Jamie sighs. 'I—'

'Don't be proud. You can pay me back later.'

Over Billy's shoulder, a very tall man is walking in, carrying a satchel and a carrier bag of baguettes. His overall look is disco backpacker—citrus neon green t-shirt underneath a sleeveless maroon pullover, shorts, walking-boots with neon coloured rolled over socks. A long, thin face on a bulbous head, accentuated by a closely shaven hairstyle—skin taut and shiny. The man cranes over Billy who's smiling unconvincingly. As the man's satchel swings forward, Jamie notices a fabric *I heart USA* badge sewn onto one of the front pockets.

'I *thought* it was you,' the man blurts, gay as a daffodil. 'I saw you as I was walking past.' He ruffles the fronds of Billy's dyed black spikes. 'How the devil are you?'

Billy angles his face to the man, who towers over him like a giant stick insect. He obviously can't remember this guy's name and Jamie enjoys letting this run on, briefly, until he weakens. 'I could wait forever for an introduction. Hi. I'm Jamie.'

'He's so rude, isn't he?' the tall man laughs. 'Matthew. Pleased to make your acquaintance.' He extends a long limp-wristed arm, hands littered with silver, slightly loose on bony fingers.

Jamie winks at Billy. 'Lovely to meet you, *Matthew*,' he says, watching Billy relax.

17

He shakes Matthew's hand and as their gazes meet, his eyes seem to move, vibrate almost, from side to side. Jamie is first to look away.

'Well, what a surprise to see you, Billy, in a vegetarian bistro, of all places. I thought you were a meat eater.'

There's an affected air about this man, behind an attempt at received pronunciation, Jamie detects an undisguisable top-note of guttural North, which brings to mind the telephone voice his mother uses to ingratiate herself with the more genteel classes, or else trying to get her own way when returning an item of silk lingerie to Marks and Spencer's.

'Room for one more?' Before Billy can reply, Matthew slides into the banquette. The waitress walks over and hands him a menu. 'I was only stopping for tea.' In the early evening sunlight, his complexion has an unnatural greenish tinge, somewhere between vomit and chlorophyll. Fresh scratches criss-cross his sinuous arm. Could he be ill? Twenty-eight? Thirty? It's not beyond comprehension. Jamie knows three men, at least, who died of AIDS in the last half year.

'Gardening,' Matthew lifts his arms. 'Bloody rose bushes.'

Jamie reproaches himself. His morbid conclusions are ignorant. Though there's something about Matthew—his clothes, his manner—unlike anyone else he's encountered.

'I finished my shift at the bakery. Just popped into the Chinese supermarket and was on my way home to cook a soup. Now I've seen you two, I might stay for a sandwich,' Matthew says. He drops his satchel and the baguettes on the floor.

'The more the merrier,' Jamie says, though Matthew strikes him as pushy. Back at the table the waitress presses a pen against a pad, waiting for them to order: sandwiches, carrot cake, coffee.

'Are we drinking?' Matthew asks. Before Jamie can mutter something about not being very flush, he produces a grating 'I'll have a dry white wine.' Jamie deduces, from Matthew's sickly sweet breath, that he's already been drinking. Matthew sucks in his cheeks and purses his lips with exaggerated feminine enthusiasm. 'Billy, do you know, I was pruning the rhododendrons the other day and it just came to me—I could see your face in my mind and I just knew we were going to bump into each other.' He pauses, draws breath and articulates his impossibly long neck. 'So Jamie, what do you do?'

Jamie searches his head for something to say, not wanting to look like a complete loser. 'I finished my fine art degree last year but now I'm focusing on my writing.'

'I'm a writer too,' Matthew says.

'Really?'

'Anything published?' Matthew asks.

'I'm working on it.'

'You're very young to be a writer. Perhaps you'll experience a bit of life first.'

'He's an apprentice,' Billy says, supportively.

'Don't mock,' Matthew says.

'I'm not.'

'Is that how your support yourself?' Jamie asks, breaking the tension.

'Well, I do a few shifts at the bakery. I don't think one needs a lot of money.'

Jamie wonders what he means by that. 'So how do you two know each other?'

Matthew looks away at Billy, tearing the corner of a paper napkin with his eyes shut. 'Long story, best left for another time,' he says.

Billy opens his eyes to Jamie. 'A while ago, before I met you.'

The smile drops from Matthew's face. 'Well, maybe it wasn't *you* I was supposed to meet that time,' he says with witchlike illumination. 'Perhaps I've been brought here for another reason. Serendipity. The universe is constantly rearranging itself.' He taps the table in front of Jamie with his forefinger. 'Do you know what I see when I look at you?'

Jamie recoils slightly at the direct challenge.

'I see a person who's afraid of life,' Matthew says, 'Afraid of letting go of the edge. But there's a great big world out there.' Matthew turns to Billy. 'Am I right?' He touches fingers to his temples and then rubs his thumbs and fingers together, as if absorbing oil into his fingertips. 'That's what I'm picking up here. You're just not living your life the way it's meant to be lived.'

'He needs a good kick up the arse,' Billy says.

'Grasp the nettle, Jamie.'

The waitress returns with food. 'You'll have to move that,' she says, sniffing at Matthew's satchel. 'It's a fire hazard.'

Matthew kicks the bag under the banquette like a rebellious

schoolboy. 'What's her problem?' He raises his hands, as if, re-sisting an invisible force field and eases them down, until they reach the table. 'I won't get annoyed. I'm just going to let this slip off me.' He turns to Jamie once more. There it is again, his eyes—vibrating from side to side. Jamie didn't imagine it this time.

'Happens to me all the time and I say to myself, "Matthew, don't get yourself involved." Because, you know, while there's all this chaos going on in the world, I'm the one who has control.'

Jamie senses Billy inwardly recoil from their new friend's hippy-dippy claptrap.

'You're an old soul. Just getting used to your new skin, aren't you?' Matthew says, regaining his genteel tone. Jamie is gripped with magnetic curiosity.

'What makes you say that?' Billy's voice has a challenging note in it.

'Vibrating on a higher frequency—more evolved,' Matthew says. 'I can feel it.' He nods at the books in front of them. 'Searching for something though. Why else would you be reading *The Prophetic Insights?*'

'Everyone's reading it,' Billy says. 'It's on special offer round the corner.'

'Isn't that fortunate?' Matthew says. 'The message is spreading far and wide.'

Billy makes yawning shapes with his mouth. 'We're trying to find Jamie somewhere to live in London.'

'Oh?' Matthew leans forward with interest.

Jamie lifts up the accommodation page in *Time Out*. 'Everything in here is way too expensive. I viewed two flea-pits in Zone Four this morning.'

'The universe provides us with everything. Just ask.' Matthew clutches empty space and makes a clenched fist in the air. 'Think of what you want. Bring it into being. Manifest!'

Jamie giggles nervously. He thinks of the poor emperor being swindled by the weavers promising to make clothes from invisible fabric and, not really knowing what to say, he takes a huge bite from his sandwich.

'Go on,' Matthew insists. 'Close your eyes and ask it.'

Jamie stares at the shape his mouth left in his sandwich, contemplating Matthew's last words. He closes his eyes and pictures himself living in London, a room of his own, traveling on the tube, making new friends. Then he opens his eyes.

'When are you thinking of coming? Matthew asks.

'As soon as possible,' Jamie says.

'If you can wait until the end of the month, I'll have a room for rent in my house. I've a flatmate moving out.'

Jamie feels his mouth open a little wider than before.

'Willesden Green—forty pounds a week. Nicely decorated. Zone Two.' Matthew makes a magician's flourish with his hands, silver rings sparkling in sunlight. 'Well, something for you to think about. You don't have to decide right now. Give me a call when you're ready?' He gets a pen from his backpack and scribbles his phone number on a serviette.

'How many flatmates do you have?' Billy asks. Jamie feels like someone has performed a card trick in front of him and he's still trying to work out the illusion.

'Well, Adrian has just gone and Mark's moving out, so there will just be me. I promised myself a bit more time on my own, but...'

They finish their sandwiches. Matthew regales them with stories of his travels across Europe before slugging back wine and announcing, 'Listen, I must go.' He drops some coins in the middle of the table. 'That should cover my order. See you both soon. Lovely to meet you, Jamie.' Matthew leans to kiss him on the cheek. *A kiss.* His large almond-shaped eyes penetrate Jamie, for a moment. 'Billy. Until next time.'

'Yes.' Billy stands to kiss him goodbye but Matthew's hand comes up evasively. 'There's absolutely no need for us to kiss.' He slips out of the banquette and pulls his satchel over his shoulder. He glances outside. 'Look at them, out there. They're running amok!' He laughs and walks out of the door.

'Did you see what he did there?' Jamie says.

'His crystal ball needs an MOT, if you ask me.'

Jamie asks the waitress for the bill, even though he can't afford to pay it. Then he turns back to Billy 'Well? *Did* you?'

'Did I what?'

'You *know*. With *him?*'

'God, of course not. He tried. I wasn't having any of it. He's bloody creepy.'

Billy counts the money Matthew left on the table and scowls.

'What's wrong?'

'He ordered *wine* and *carrot cake*. There's about enough money here to pay for half a sandwich. Self-seeking fucker.'

'That's not very spiritual,' Jamie says.

Billy holds up Matthew's telephone number. 'Still, looks like you've got your accommodation sorted out.'

Jamie pulls a face. 'Move in with someone I just met in a coffee shop? What would Mum think?'

§

Jamie raps the front window of his nan's house and presses his face against the glass. On the other side, Phyllis lifts net curtain up. 'Oh, look at ya! Get yer nose off the glass, varmint! I've only just cleaned them windows.' She lets the net drop and, in a few seconds, Jamie can hear her turning a key inside. He steps towards the front door, set within a rendering of ugly raspberry-ripple pebbledash, as it is flung open.

'Get in here—pest!' Phyllis says, wiping her glasses on her pinnie.

Jamie looks past her and into the living room. The TV is on and Uncle Freddie and Auntie Sandra are slouched on the sofa. 'Hello everyone,' Jamie says, walking in past Phyllis who is standing in the hallway. 'I'm glad you two are here. I've just come to say I'm—'

'You've come just in time,' Sandra says, waving a small piece of pink paper at him and pointing to the telly. On the screen, Dale Winton is hosting the *National Lottery* programme; he's protesting fey straightness and pretending to flirt with his guests, *The Spice Girls*. Jamie leans and kisses his Auntie on the cheek. Her hair has been freshly highlighted and she smells of perfume.

'Alright, our Jamie,' Freddie says, warmly. 'Got yer ticket?'

Jamie feels nan's hand in the small of his back, pushing him further into the room. He breathes in deeply, and savours the soothing essence of home. The comfortable feeling he gets from being in this room makes him wonder if he's doing the right thing. There has been lots of laughs in this room. There has been Christmas parties and birthday parties, engagement parties and anniversaries. For a second, Jamie imagines the room dressed with balloons and streamers. Whatever the occasion, there would always be a *nice spread* put on by nan—beef paste sandwiches, pickled onions and cheese on sticks, pieces of Battenberg, mandarins suspended in orange jelly, cucumber slices swimming in vinegar, that sort of fare. Wouldn't he miss all that? Then noticing the other armchair, empty, 'No Grandad?' he asks.

'He's up in his shed,' Phyllis says. 'Best place for him. He's been getting on my bleedin' nerves today.'

'It would be nice if he could be here to hear what I've got to say.' There has been so many events at Nan's house, they all blur into one. As Jamie looks around the room, the vibrations of those fond moments still echo around this space, the place where people people know him and care for him.

'Sounds ominous,' Freddie says. 'If you've come to tell us that you're going to wear women's clothes and start calling your-self Doris, think on Jamie. Your grandad's still getting his head round the last revelation, relic that he is.' Jamie is reminded that some people don't know him at all. 'What is it now, Nancy Boy?' Freddie giggles.

Sandra cracks him over the head with the back of her hand. 'What have you been told about using that word?' she says, leaving Freddie wincing and rubbing the side of his head.

'Leave Alf where he is, Jamie. He's giving us all a break,' Phyllis says. 'Do you want a cup of tea, our Jamie?'

'No thanks, Nan. I'm not thirsty.'

Sandra sits forward in her seat and frowns. 'I hope this is not going to take long, Jamie. They're going to call the numbers in a few minutes. I want to win. Freddie's got his heart set on a fancy holiday to Torremolinos next year.'

Phyllis settles herself into her arm chair and picks up her knitting. Jamie remembers how he used to sit next to her while she taught him to knit, a plate of biscuits with cheese and pic-calilli balanced between them. She taught him well—all the stitches, casting on and casting off. He could even follow a sim-ple pattern. He's never dropped the habit. He always has his knitting with him on a journey or when he's away from home. More often than not, he'll just knit long lengths of yarn in the shape of a scarf. He finds it therapeutic—a way of switching off from the world. 'Right, hurry up and spill, Posh's going to *release the balls* in a minute and I need to get the back of this cardigan finished.' She inserts her knitting needle into the first stitch and then she's off—fingers working autonomously as the loops of wool slide from on needle to another.

Jamie takes a deep breath and says, 'I'm going back to London, tomorrow.'

Phyllis nods. 'Oh, that'll be nice for you. Trip away. See your mates—'

'No. Not a trip, Nan. I'm going back to live.'

Phyllis' fingers slow down but they do not stop working. 'What? I thought you were going to settle round here for a bit, get a job, see a bit more of your old nan?'

'He don't wanna be stuck round here, Mother,' Sandra intervenes. 'He's young. He wants to be amongst his people. He wants to be where it's all happening, don't you, Bab?'

'I miss it, Nan. An opportunity came up and I decided—'

'Right, it's starting.' Sandra's eyes have become super-glued to the television screen. 'They're doing it now, Mum! Shhhssshh.'

'I'll be back to visit you all,' Jamie says. 'It's only a few hours on the train. And you can come and see me.' Jamie sits on the arm of Phyllis' chair.

'*Release the balls*,' Sandra roars and titters to herself. She and Freddie cling to each other with excitement. 'Right, don't speak. Don't speak.'

'It's a bit sudden, isn't it, Jamie? It only seems five minutes since you've been back. What's with the itchy feet?'

'Twenty-nine!' Sandra shrieks. 'I've got one. I've got one.'

'It's nothing personal, Nan. There's nothing for me round here.'

'Thirty-three! Another one!' Sandra squeals. 'How many have you got, Freddie?'

Jamie looks down at Phyllis. Her knitting has come off the needles. 'Now look what I've gone and done.' She looks up at him and shakes her head. 'Jamie, I need new glasses. I just can't see properly anymore. I'll never be able to get this back on the needles.'

'Oh Nan, be careful, don't let it run.' Jamie carefully takes the length of knitting out of her hands. 'Let's have a look. I'll sort this.' Jamie replaces the stitches, one by one, back onto the needles. He checks the tension and knits two rows of stitches to ensure the piece is still intact. Then he hands the knitting back to Phyllis. 'There, I've done one row of knit and one row of purl. Back to knit now.'

'You are a kind boy,' Phyllis says.

Freddie snorts. 'Nancy,' he says out of the side of his mouth.

Phyllis' eyes lock on to him. 'Do you want me to put my toe up your behind? Mark my words, I will!'

'Well, a bloke of his age. Knitting!'

'What are you scoffing for, you useless bugger. It's a very good skill to have. You never know, it might save his life one day. You can't even change a bloody lightbulb.'

'Arseholes,' Sandra spits. 'Looks like it'll have to be another bloody weekend in Rhyl.'

§

'A complete stranger!' Gloria's voice cracks into falsetto as she parts the curls of her hair, pressing them against her head revealing the dark rootage, in the little mirror inside her sunshield—bloody hell, must get it done.

Roy nudges her knee, which, resting against his gear stick, is preventing him from changing down as they reach the end of the motorway in North-West London. 'We're almost there, Glo. It's a bit late to talk him out of it now, don't you think?'

In the back, Jamie sighs. 'You've decided you don't like him before you've even met him.'

Gloria rubs away smudged mascara with the tip of her index finger. 'Honestly Roy, he hasn't been this much trouble since he brought home that dried snake skin from Paul Fullbrook's house and left it in my side of the bed. Jamie, I don't like this. It's history repeating itself.'

'I'm not doing this to hurt you, Mother.'

That look again in the mirror. 'You're not in love with him, are you?' she asks, flipping his reflection against the upholstered ceiling of the car.

'You know, if you gave Matthew a chance, you might even get to like him. He's travelled—speaks different languages. I could learn from him. He's amazing.'

'Oh, well I can't wait to meet this *amazing* person—'

She turns to her son, suspiciously. He's wearing clothes she's never seen him in before—a black woollen cap and a second-hand sheepskin jacket. Looks like something from *Fiddler of the Roof.* 'Where did you get that coat?'

'Matthew gave it to me.'

'Dressing you now, is he?'

Roy wrenches open the glove compartment and pulls out an A-Z. 'I'm going to need you to navigate from here, Glo. I've put a bookmark in the right page for you.'

'People move in with strangers all the time,' Jamie says. 'They find them in newspapers, on postcards in shop windows…'

'I've never heard the like.' As they shuttle forward towards a slowing car in front of them, Gloria's right leg reaches for an imaginary brake pedal. 'Roy, you're going a bit quick, aren't you?' She covers her eyes, peeping through splayed fingers.

Jamie says, 'It's all about control with you, isn't it?'

The car radio crackles and the dour voice of a BBC newsreader makes yet another announcement of the death of Princess Diana. They've been occurring periodically since the car crash in the early hours of the morning. Gloria can't help thinking of the sons Diana has left behind.

'Roy, speak to him, please!'

'Don't bring me into it,' Roy says. 'He's old enough and ugly enough to make his own mistakes.'

Gloria changes tack. 'How will you support yourself?' she snaps.

'I've got a job. You know the supermarket gave me a transfer and—'

'A transfer? You talk about it like you have an executive job in The City. Is that why you studied for three years—so you could wear a little blue waistcoat and sit on a supermarket checkout?'

'*You* work in a shop!' Jamie retorts.

'I've got your dad.'

'Some people don't even have or need jobs.'

'Oh, here we go! What type of people, Jamie? *Alternative* people? Or are you referring to those lazy bloody slobs conning the arse out of the country? I brought you up to stand on your own two feet.'

'You know what your problem is, Mother?'

'Pray tell.'

'Your need for protection is so great that you build up a wall. You cling to what you know. You hate change. You hate difference. You're threatened by anything new, anything you don't understand and you won't allow it in. You look down your bloody nose at everyone. But instead of feeling more secure, you'll be alone.'

'I didn't raise you to speak to me like this.'

Roy over-revs the engine at Neasden Junction and weaves, aggressively, across four indistinct lanes of kamikaze traffic. 'Will you pair just give it a rest!'

This time Gloria presses both feet into the footwell. 'Bloody hell, Roy.' She flings the A-Z at Jamie and continues to work her way through the packet of stomach settlers she'd started at Milton Keynes whilst Jamie reads directions. But Roy manages mainly on his own, treasure that he is. He'd studied the map as if revising for an exam before the journey.

As they pull up outside Matthew's house, Gloria turns and asks, 'Did you remember to pack your toothbrush?'

'Yes, Mum.' Jamie scowls.

'And a flannel?'

Roy shakes his head at her, 'Muzzle it, would you?' he says. 'Come on, Sunshine. Let's get your things.'

Gloria looks up at the Edwardian house, rather looming and imperious for a modest suburban semi-detached. Something about its miniature turrets and grinning bay window give it its own devious personality. A tall man is standing at the front door in shorts and a torn shirt. He's holding a small gardening fork. That must be him, watching her as she adjusts her blouse. Look at him! Gloria gets out of the car and rushes up to Jamie and speaks in his ear. 'Don't be walking around barefoot, our Jamie. Got to be careful. Hypodermic needles!'

'Gloria!' Roy barks. She's overstepped the mark. 'Behave yourself and grab hold of this.' Roy swings a suitcase at her and, as he lets go of the handle, the dead weight of it almost pulls her over.

Jamie, ahead of her, is first at the door. 'Hello, Matthew,' he says, quietly. Gloria watches their smiles of allegiance as Jamie passes into the hallway.

'Dump your cases there,' Matthew says, pointing to a spot at the foot of the stairs. 'I can help you unpack your things later. I'll make a pot of tea.'

'Oh, good. I'm parched.' Gloria reaches the front door. 'Gloria,' she says, straining with the large suitcase. She drops it at Matthew's feet. Useless bugger!

'You must be Jamie's mum,' Matthew says. 'I love what you're wearing.'

A little flattered, she laughs. 'Oh, how kind of you to say!'

'I love that colour. It's quite nutty. Would you say that's grey or beige.'

'It's taupe.' She steps in through the door and moves to stand next to Jamie.

'I'll get that, shall I?' Matthew says, lifting the case across the threshold and placing it at the foot of the stairs. He then holds up his hands, fingernails caked with soil. 'Spot of gardening, Gloria. Won't shake your hand.'

She's relieved. 'My feet are throbbing. Just let me sit down.'

'Don't mind her,' Jamie says. 'She's a martyr to her swollen ankles.'

Gloria cracks him across the back of the head and he lets out a voiceless, embarrassed squeal. 'Been asking for that all morning, cheeky swine.'

She's alarmed by Matthew—so tall and gaunt. 'Jamie hasn't stopped talking about you,' she says, forcing a show of niceness. 'I've been waiting to see what all the fuss is about.'

'Only good things, I hope,' Matthew says, in a posh accent but Gloria can see through it. Got a lot of shit on him.

'This is my husband, Roy,' she says, proudly.

Roy sticks out his hand. Matthew raises soiled hands again. 'How was the journey?'

Roy pauses heavily.

'We made good time,' Gloria answers for him. 'The traffic got a bit busier as we came into London but the motorway was relatively clear.' She tilts her head at Roy, apologetically.

'Go on through,' Matthew lifts a third suitcase into the house. Roy hesitates, steps inside, closes the door firmly behind him and stands for a long moment in the hallway, motionless, eyes fixed on one of those brightly coloured Sacred Heart images that Gloria once spotted in a street market in Alicante. Now that the daylight has been blocked out it's possible to see candles flickering. Roy's face is lit up; his nose is wrinkled like the arse end of a cooked chicken, detecting what Gloria has already spotted—a burning stick of some scented rubbish.

Matthew points to a room off the hallway. 'Make yourselves at home.' He disappears into the kitchen.

Gloria doesn't move from her spot. What a dump! The hallway walls have been stripped bare, washed in some sort of transparent brown muck with a gloss surface. This has left them with a fake medieval appearance—the kind she's seen on TV in those ridiculous makeover programmes. A thick red bell rope accessorizes the banister, leading to a candlelit upstairs. Gothic candelabras and Moroccan tea lights illuminate the downstairs area. The only other decorations are a cluster of gaudy Jesus or Mary pictures spread throughout the hall and stairwell. One large Sacred Heart takes pride of place above the telephone table and a pile of directories. Her eyes come back to Matthew, sashaying from the kitchen with a tray. Look at the colour of him. Doesn't look well.

Matthew clears his throat, perhaps annoyed to find them all still standing in the hall. 'Tea,' he says vividly, and ushers them all past an empty room that Gloria has already guessed will be Jamie's, into the living room. 'Please, take a seat—'

'Forgot to pay the electric?' There's no shortage of candelabra, even though this seems to be the side of the house that catches the afternoon sun. Coloured stalactites and stalagmites of candle wax have collected on wrought ironwork and parquet flooring.

Gloria heads to a large patio window and peers out. Polythene bags of soil lie around on the flagstones. A compost heap at the rear of the garden harbours fresh scraps of carrot and orange peel.

Matthew is arranging cups and saucers on the dining table. Well at least he makes tea properly, with a teapot. She'll give him that.

'Milk and sugar?' Matthew asks.

'Milk for me, please. Neither for Roy; he's being careful.'

The Earl Grey tea he pours only succeeds in increasing Roy's stiffness. He can't stand that bloody scented muck. And Jamie sits fidgeting on the sofa, probably embarrassed that his parents are even here. He might be in his early twenties, but in reality, look at him: still a kid with a ridiculous bleached mop and a t-shirt she'd only ironed for him this morning. Matthew won't get his whites *that* white.

Gloria makes an effort to keep conversation going. 'Lovely garden. Roy loves gardening, don't you Roy?' Conversation isn't Roy's thing at the best of times, unless coaxed out of him with a bit of boiled ham.

'It's my pride and joy,' Matthew says.

'Roy's just installed a pond in ours. He deliberated for some time over whether to put in a preformed fibreglass pool or use a liner. In the end, he went for a liner. Such a perfectionist, my husband.'

Finally, she sits down next to Roy on the sofa. 'So this is *your* house?' she asks, locking eyes with Matthew.

'It's my *home*,' Matthew says.

'And what are you charging him?'

'Mother! That's my business.' Jamie looks aghast.

'Forty pounds a week,' Matthew says.

Jamie tuts.

'Well I suppose he'll just afford that on his wages from the *supermarket*, won't he?' she says, spite getting the better of her. 'But he won't be here for long. I expect he and Billy will want to get a place of their own.'

'There you go again,' Jamie says. 'Making decisions for me.'

'Thank you.' Gloria takes a teacup. She slurps on tea, hiding her displeasure at its funny taste. 'Dreadful shame about Diana, eh?' she hurries along. 'I suppose it will hit you Londoners hard.'

Matthew looks at her, quizzically, for a moment, as if he's misheard. 'Yes, I suppose it will. But I'm—'

'Not a real Londoner?'

'No,' Matthew says emphatically, as if stamping his foot. 'Not a fan of royalty.'

'Are you not? We've got a lovely commemorative wedding mug. Who would have thought it would end up like this?'

Matthew averts his eyes. He's got something to hide; Gloria knows it. She feels the skin on her face tightening—perhaps the beginning of a hot flush. They have been coming more frequently lately. She bit the postman's head off the other day just for walking on the lawn.

'So where are you from, originally?'

He deigns to lift his eyes again to look at her. 'Sheffield. But I haven't been back for years.'

'I'm sure it will be a kick in the teeth for some people,' she says.

'Sorry?'

'Diana. I mean the papers thrived off her.' She finishes her tea.

'Gosh, you can drink it *that* hot?' Matthew says.

'Asbestos mouth,' she says. 'Right then. We'll be off. If I can just use your loo.'

'Top of the stairs, first door on your right.'

She points a forefinger at Roy. 'Hurry up and finish your tea.' She leaves them in silence. When she reaches the top of the stairs, the floorboards creak on a hexagonal landing stinking of incense. The walls upstairs are covered with more of those kitsch pictures of Jesus. The landing has five open doors off it. Three bedrooms, a bathroom and a toilet hardly big enough to sit down in.

There's a high-level cistern with a flush handle on a rusty chain. A smell of damp reminds her of the cold outside khazi she'd used as a child, where she discovered her first period.

The interior of Matthew's loo has been entirely pasted over with cuttings of news photos from the Eastern Bloc. Shirtless Soviet boy soldiers, flaunting themselves in front of the camera, feature dominantly. The pictures have been varnished flat to the plaster. Who in their right mind does this to a perfectly good wall? Why would her son want to stay here, of all places, with this man—a cross between ET and Peter O'Toole?

She closes the door—no latch, flicks her clothes up out of the way, squats over the toilet seat without actually making contact—a practise she's rehearsed many times. Thighs trembling, she reaches forward with one hand to hold the door closed and pees. She checks the seat for dribble and flushes. The bottom of the toilet bowl is covered in a thick layer of lime-scale, in dire need of a bottle of bleach. And a crack! A cracked seat harbours germs. She leaves the toilet and walks into the bathroom to wash her hands. *It's my home.* Home? What the hell does that mean? It's a bloody squat. That's what it is. A *squat*. No bloody wallpaper, no carpets anywhere, nails sticking out of floors. She looks at the bath, which has a tidemark running all the way around it and a plughole bunged up with the tiny bits of soap and hair. No towel. She wipes her hands on her jeans.

On the landing, one of the doors is ajar. Creeping about, trying to avoid squeaky floorboards, she sees clothes on the floor and the starry edge of an American flag on the wall. But that's all. She hasn't the nerve to pry, even though she wants to turn the place over and find evidence that Matthew is a total creep.

Trailing a finger along the banister, she descends, breathing sharply through clamped teeth. 'Dirt,' she whispers. Then her eyes come back to Matthew, waiting at the foot of the stairs. I know what *you* are, she thinks—eco warrior, *never-paid-national insurance*, dog-on-a-rope sort. That's what you are.

'You ready, love?' Roy asks, man of so many words.

She looks directly ahead at the door in the hallway they'd missed earlier.

Matthew opens it. 'This will be Jamie's room,' he says, reassuringly.

She pokes her nose around the door. Clean and tidy, at least. *No curtains.* No furniture—just a bed and a clothes rail.

'You'll have to get some nets put up those windows.'

'I'll be alright, Mum. I'll sort it.'

This doesn't feel right at all. Jamie wouldn't come back with them, even if she demanded. He'd dig his heels in. It's enough, for now, that Matthew knows she doesn't trust him. But she'll be there, when it all goes wrong. Because it will, won't it?

Turning at the door, she hugs Jamie. 'Call us as soon as you've got yourself settled in.'

'Yes. I will. I'll wave to you from the bedroom window,' he says and retreats inside.

Roy looks at Matthew smiling down on him. 'Well, nice to meet you, fella.'

'Good to meet you too,' Matthew says. Roy jangles his car keys and walks off down the driveway.

Gloria can feel herself lingering slightly—one leg on the driveway going after Roy, the other straddling the doorstep. She turns back into the doorway and Matthew fills her vision—too close—close enough that she can smell his offensive breath. And *Oh my God! What's wrong with his eyes?*

'It's time to let go now, Gloria. He's a big boy.'

She's intimidated, caught adrift from Jamie and Roy. He's one of those sexual ones—a predator. If he so much as lays a finger on her son she'll—

She eyeballs him, making sure he looks away first. She lets go of the doorframe and walks away.

From inside the car, Gloria fights back tears and waves to Jamie, standing at his bedroom window, as Roy accelerates away.

'Well, that was bloody awkward,' Roy says.

'It's not right. I'm always right about my instincts—as you well know.' She touches him on the leg, reminding herself of the familiarity they share. 'Get us home.'

§

Truth be told, Jamie's glad to see the back of them. For the first time since they'd set off this morning, there's a space in his head where Gloria's voice had been.

In his new bedroom, he hangs the last of his pitiful assortment of clothes on the rail: a jacket, and checking the pockets, finds a little piece of paper inside it.

I love you, Soft Lad.

He smiles. He hasn't worn this jacket since the last time he saw Billy. It's the fifth one he's found today—one inside his shoe. *I miss you.* One was inside the chest pocket of a shirt, one inside the zipper of his suitcase and another inside his jeans. This is Billy—little gestures of kindness.

'Are you hungry?' Matthew's voice echoes from the kitchen.

Jamie can hear his music—a minimalist classical arrangement with lots of bells and strings. Jamie loves it. The rest of his belongings are on the floor, along with his well-thumbed copy of *The Prophetic Insights*. Matthew's sorted out some nets *to put up the windows*. His mother was, in fact, correct; the window exposes the room to the whole street.

'Starving.'

'It's Thai. Trust me, this is going to be delicious.'

'I'll be right in.' He makes the bed, checks himself in front of a glass mirror, leaning against the lilac anaglypta. There are two versions of himself: the one in his mind's eye, the shy schoolboy always covering up, aping some idealistic notion of heterosexuality. Look where that had got him—fondled by lonely, desperate middle-aged women at parties. The other version, staring back at him from the mirror, is altogether different to Jamie Johnson of the West Midlands. This is the type of gent he hopes would stand out in the crowd. His parents accept the gay thing, in their own way. You're alright if you're like them—settle down, spend Sunday afternoons shopping for garden sheds in B & Q. But, Jamie wants to be *queer*—a word his mother thinks is rude and distasteful. He imagines Billy in his student lodgings, surrounded by photographs by Mapplethorpe and books about Jarman.

When he enters the living room, Matthew is absent. The table is set. Candles are lit, flames flickering with the gentle breeze from the open patio window. A large steaming saucepan of green broth sits alongside glasses and a bottle of fizzy wine. Jamie edges further into the room toward the wide sliding door. Just outside, a couple of planters with masses of flowers are made visible in the spill of light from inside. Beyond that it's dark. Jamie finds the switch for the garden lights.

He calls out into the night, 'Matthew?' He moves closer to the window, his feet touching the lip of the window frame, eyes becoming accustomed to the darkness. A ghostly outline is visible, arms outstretched, at the top of the garden, only metres away.

'What are you doing?' Jamie whispers. Matthew spins, like a child deliberately trying to make himself sick. Round and round—counting his revolutions, 'One hundred and six... One hundred and seven... one hundred and eight... one hundred and nine...'

Jamie watches with red-faced confusion—he might as well have caught him masturbating. Matthew stumbles giddily for a moment. Jamie scuttles back to the dining table and pretends to be arranging place settings.

When Matthew flounces back in. 'Do the honours!'

Jamie wonders what he means?

'The wine! Let's pop.' Matthew laughs.

'I love the music,' Jamie says.

'Philip Glass.'

Jamie smiles and marks a few notes in the air with his fingers. 'She's ever so uptight, isn't she?'

'Who?'

'Your mother.' Matthew sits down to stir the soup. 'She needs to loosen up,' he says, apparently finding great amusement in this idea. He sucks in his cheeks and flares the whites of his eyes in a pretentious, self-important gesture. Then Matthew softens. He must have noticed Jamie bristle. 'My parents are the same.' Jamie can't imagine Matthew's mother is anything like his own.

Jamie pops the cork and sprays them both with Cava, provoking a little squeal from Matthew who claps his hands together. He pours two glasses. 'She's not all that bad,' Jamie says.

'Don't get me wrong. Gloria's a beautiful human being. But Jamie, all mothers have to let go at some point, even yours.'

They drink and talk over dinner—Matthew's love of throbbing techno, favourite films and where Jamie can go out in this part of London. Jamie's never tasted Thai food before. The soup has an unusual flavour. Like everything around him now, he's not sure if he likes it or not, but it makes a refreshing change from Gloria's traditional English roasts.

Matthew's voice grows ever grander. 'It was Caribbean and Creole food when I was a child. Dad liked roast beef and Yorkshire pudding but that would only happen if he cooked it himself. Mother insisted on traditional cooking.' Matthew gazes into the middle distance for a moment.

'You never say much about your parents,' Jamie enquires.

'What's happened to the lovely Billy?'

'Didn't think you'd appreciate me inviting guests so soon.'

'I thought he'd be over to christen that bed in there.'

Jamie looks into his soup. He examines the ingredients before ladling another spoonful into his mouth. Chilli, ginger and green peas are about all he recognizes.

'All good stuff. Lemongrass, galangal, pak-choi... And some spirulina.'

'What's *spirulina*?' Jamie asks.

'Micro-algae from deep under the ocean. Boosts the immune system.'

Jamie remarks that he'd once read a book all about a woman who, riddled with cancer, had healed herself by altering her diet and remodelling her thought processes. When the doctors tested her, the cancer had not only gone into remission but had disappeared entirely.

'The mind is a very powerful thing,' Matthew says.

Jamie's eyes fall on a row of large photograph albums lined up on the floor, each spine labelled with marker pen: *Berlin, Bucharest, Thailand, Auschwitz, Moscow, Kosovo* and *Moldova*.

'I'm envious of your travelling,' Jamie says.

'You'll do it too.' Matthew gulps down wine. 'Just as soon as you start living your life instead of letting your mother live it for you.'

Jamie grasps the wine now and pours himself a large one.

§

'Stop the car, Roy.' Gloria's voice rises above a passing police siren.

'What now? We're nearly home.'

'Stop the fucking car!'

Roy swings into a roadside layby and skids to a standstill, tyres spitting up gravel. 'Jesus, Glo!'

'You're freaking me out, Roy. All this time I've been going along with it because you're the rational one. And now you say *you're* not comfortable.' She's unravelling, like rows and rows of stitches free of knitting needles. 'We've dropped off our son in a house worthy of Norman Bates and just left him there.'

'Gloria, I don't like it any more than you do.' Roy has always had a brand of non-stick robustness that made her feel secure, like *Teflon* or *Kevlar*. The world is always all fine because Roy is there—as sure as the tide comes in. But here, now, his voice has a note of uncertainty. 'If I thought we could change his mind, I'd turn around right now.'

'I'm living on my nerves, I am,' Gloria says. 'We've bought our Jamie up in a decent house, with decent things, to live a decent life. And now this! Oh, it doesn't bode well. Roy? Are you listening to me? This isn't like that time he decided to give up eating meat and start growing his own vegetables. This is something else. Something's going to happen. It's like he's under a spell! And now he's even wearing Matthew's clothes. The look that *thing* gave me when we were leaving —'

45

'Gloria, let's not turn this into something that it's not.' Roy squeezes her hand tightly.

'And if you'd heard the way he spoke to me. He's got breath the kind you'd back away from holding a crucifix.'

'What do you want me to do—put him in a straightjacket?'

She looks at her fingers—chipped polish. 'My nails won't take this, Roy.'

§

'Moldova?' Jamie ponders a topic of conversation that will a) not reveal himself to be a complete idiot and b) elevate him, in Matthew's eyes, to protégé status. He's thinking of the photo albums in the living room, where Matthew is stalking with an incense stick like a witch doctor exorcising evil spirits as Jamie squirts washing-up liquid into a sink filling with hot water—something chemical free and environmentally friendly. Submerging plates and cutlery into bubbles, he smiles at the decadent contrast between the elegant cut-glass in his hands and the uneven stone floor of the kitchen—appliances askew like listing boats in a harbour.

He closes his eyes and pushes his hands down into the comforting warm water. Ah. This house pulsates with exotic aromas. Colours and stylish embellishments clash everywhere he looks. There's still the trace of something in his mouth. What did Matthew call it? His mother's never heard of coriander, let alone introduced it into her cooking.

They'll be arguing over something by now… Should they have a water-feature in the fish pond? Or, whether to set the table for dinner or have it on a tray in front of the telly—those sorts of really important conversations.'

'Sorry, didn't catch that.'

Jamie opens his eyes. 'It's an unusual place to visit.' Geography was never his strong point.

Matthew discards the incense. 'Well, in those days, you could buy a train ticket that would get you thousands of miles across Europe. I was halfway across Romania when I met a young couple who'd been travelling the same way. We befriended each other. They were heading for a town near the border. I forget the name of it. Call me naïve, but it wasn't until the last minute I realized we were entering a conflict zone. I saw roadside graves and a roadblock.' Matthew pauses dramatically, as he puts the kettle on.

'I just knew if I did the wrong thing, or said the wrong thing they'd shoot me. I mean these guys weren't messing around. They took my luggage and smashed my camera. I'd been really foolish. I was going to have to be very clever if I was going to get out of such a dangerous situation.' Matthew's voice grows low and dark—a master of storytelling. 'So I just spoke very calmly. I didn't want to piss them off. They kept me in a shed near the roadside for a couple of days. No proper buildings. Strip-searched me and took my clothes away. They just shouted at me in pidgin English. The soldiers kept touching me, pushing me around. At one point I thought they would rape me, but they didn't. I knew I couldn't descend into that. I knew I had to banish those thoughts.'

'You must have been terrified,' Jamie says.

'Naturally. They interrogated me for days.' Matthew continues tea making. 'I think it was all about massaging their egos, making them feel powerful. I was their toy, you see. Somehow, I just managed to talk myself out of the situation. Strength of mind,' Matthew says, his voice brightening. 'They let me go because of who I am.'

Jamie wipes the kitchen surfaces and lets his dripping hands fall to his sides. 'What do you mean, *because of who you are?*'

'I knew that if I could survive that experience, I could get through anything.' Matthew lifts teacups. Jamie follows him through the dining room towards the garden. 'It was very liberating.'

'Look at this,' Matthew says, lifting up a postcard he spotted on his way through the living room—an advertisement for a New-Age convention called *Anything is Possible.* 'I picked it up the other day, in the esoteric shop I like to visit. It spoke to me. Like, *I'm for Jamie.*'

Jamie smiles. 'Shall we go?'

'Anything is possible.'

The sky in Welston would be black and prickled with white dots. Here the stars are lost behind a viscosity of light pollution. The moon, though, is bright and large. In the dilute light, Matthew's face looks otherworldly, as he stares up at it. 'Ask the universe…'

Jamie says, 'Can I ask *you* something?'

'You can ask me anything.'

'Why do you collect those pictures of Jesus?'

§

'Look at all these,' There's a bread-crate outside the *Scan'n'Pack* full of discarded sandwiches. 'It's the universe at work.' Matthew picks it up. 'That's dinner sorted out.'

Jamie's phone rings. 'Oh, please come tonight,' Jamie starts immediately before Billy can get a word in edgeways. 'We've hardly seen each other this week.'

'If you will insist I come to that house.'

'It's where I live!'

'Will *he* be there?' Billy asks.

'Of course.'

'He's a freak.'

Jamie looks at Matthew, handing out sandwiches to a homeless guy sitting on the pavement. 'Not from where I'm standing.'

§

Jamie lurches after Matthew up the steps of Shoreditch Town Hall and into the Gilbert and George art opening, tipsy from the bottle of cava they'd guzzled on the journey. Jamie's excited to see that Matthew knows *everyone*. In a film-star entrance of mouthed helllloooos, Matthew gestures to people on the other side of the hall, well-known members of the art world—the 'Bitterati' he calls them. Jamie recognizes faces he's only ever seen on the covers of magazines and on television—Andrew Logan, Philip Salon—groups of freaks in flamboyant attire and fantasy make-up and his hero, Boy George, whose appearance leaves him speechless. It's almost as if Jamie has seen... a unicorn.

'I can't believe I'm here,' Jamie says.

At the edge of the crowd, Matthew turns. He presses his hands onto Jamie's shoulders. 'Do you mean to say you wanted to be *anywhere* else? Don't underestimate yourself, Jamie. Only *you* could have brought this into being.'

Jamie nods. 'The universe provides us with everything we need.'

Matthew smiles back at him—his unearthly almond-shaped eyes, unblinking hazel rimmed with blue. 'You're very special, Jamie.'

He leads Jamie by the hand across the room. 'So many people I want you to meet—David, Gracie... so many people.'

Within minutes Matthew is holding court. 'I thought I was going to die,' he says to a fixated crowd, mouths agape.

'Oh, that's terrible.'

'How did you get away?'

'You must have been terrified.'

Matthew appears to be devouring every second of it, perhaps making a meal of it for Jamie's benefit. 'Take it from me, if it hadn't been for my strength of character, I might not be alive now.' Jamie wonders if the god complex Matthew developed as a child had really gone for good: are those religious icons back at the house simply souvenirs from an angst ridden adolescence or does he believe he really *is* Jesus Christ reincarnated?

Beside Jamie, a handsome man in lederhosen seems to be enjoying the story. 'Hi, I'm Jamie,' Jamie says, suddenly conscious of his supermarket uniform. 'I'm a friend of Matthew.'

The man's smile drops. 'Oh, really?' He moves away.

Amongst the throng is a man who Matthew is keen for Jamie to meet. He's been dubbed as being all glamour and no shame— performance artist, costume designer and club host—Bond villain minus the pussy. He's staring. A bleached platinum quiff with a subtle lilac rinse is set off by a navy 1940s double-breasted suit, over a ruffled shirt. He sidles up, wiggling his fingers inside lilac silk gloves.

'David. David Cabaret,' he says. 'Wonderful to make your acquaintance.' He drags out the vowels in exaggerated feminine abandon as he takes Jamie's hand in his own and kisses it.

Matthew can be heard over the buzz of the room. 'We're all connected, everyone. Take it from me. We're all from the stars.'

David rolls his eyes and whispers into Jamie's ear, 'Take no notice. He talks a load of old shit.' He drains his glass through a straw and dumps it, as if needing both hands for a fight. Then he looks coquettishly at Jamie, from behind lilac contact lenses. 'Come on, *you*!' David tugs Jamie's sleeve. 'You can get me a drink.' Jamie steps back and presses his hands against empty pockets, feeling for coins.

'It's an art opening, daaarling! No-one pays for the drinks,' David says, grasping two glasses of bubbly from a passing waiter.

Relieved, Jamie sighs and accepts one from him. 'I love your outfit.'

'Oh, this old thing.' David holds out his sleeves, pretending to brush a bit of dust from them. 'Well, it'll do for these two—' he says, motioning to Gilbert and George who are holding court on the balcony. 'I usually make more of an effort.' David does a little twirl. 'Tell me you're not one of his conquests.'

Jamie touches his forehead, drawing a blank.

'Pinocchio, over there,' David nods in Matthew's direction.

'Oh, no. He's my housemate. I already have a boyfriend.' Jamie scans the room again. Boy George has vanished and there's no sign of Billy either.

David looks around. 'He's not here?'

'No. Not yet.'

David purses his lips. 'My lucky night then. Oh look, there's Princess Julia and…' He stands brazenly pointing and reels off a list of names, some of whom Jamie recognises as veterans of 80s London club society, Blitz Kids and 'faces' of Leigh Bowery's infamous Soho nightclub, *Taboo*. 'There's Molly Parkin and Mr Pearl and there's—Oh! God! Isn't! He! Lovely! Michael Clark the dancer, I-made-a-costume-for-him… and oh, look there's—'

David shifts from side to side, annoyed by the crowd obstructing his line of vision to a young man in a white vest and jeans, revealing a chest inked with William Morris tattoos.

Hypnotised by the man's beauty, Jamie wobbles. 'Who is that?' he whispers.

'That's Simon Jones.' David licks his lips.

There's still no sign of Billy. The last time they'd seen each other there had been an unexplained distance, into which Jamie had read a need for Billy to untangle himself. Jamie also suspected he'd smelt someone else's aftershave on Billy's neck.

David licks a finger and rubs a stain on the cuff of his jacket. 'You made this?' Jamie asks.

'Of course. This jacket got me on the pages of all the scene magazines,' David says in a fit of unbridled flounce. 'I make all my own costumes. I'm just *fabulous*.'

A voice booms from behind them. 'All the fun-fur in the world won't make *you* fabulous, David Cabaret!' They spin. A helmet of bleached white hair with darker dyed layers beneath, pussyfoots towards them. She arcs her cigarillo, turning the art of smoking into a ballet. Her 60s feline eyes are the result of expertly applied shadow and liquid liner.

David gasps, 'Gracie Sharp! Speak of the devil and she shall—'

'Davey-baby. Long-time-no-see. Where have you been, you little recluse?' Gracie's voice is deep enough to be a touch masculine. Dusty Springfield—but with finer features and flawless skin. The rest is a black kaftan affair with black culottes.

'It's been all go,' David replies. 'London Fashion Week and all.'

'*You* need to get out more, David. People will forget who you are.'

'Me. Nooo,' he roars at her.

'You want to be a *has been*?'

Jamie plucks up the courage to tell Gracie, 'You look amazing.'

'It's all drag, baby,' she says, throwing a limp hand at him. She draws the last puff from her cigarillo and drops it into David's empty glass.

'Charming.' David tuts.

Gracie turns her attention to Jamie. 'Oh David, isn't he just sweetness personified? I could eat him.'

Jamie feels himself blush.

'Bring me a knife and fork,' David says.

Gracie squeezes her eyelids together. 'So how do you know David?'

'We only met tonight. I know Matthew.' Jamie indicates his gangly-legged friend. 'He's a friend of David.'

Her face is fixed, as if someone has pressed a pause button. '*Is* he a friend?'

'*I* didn't invite him,' David says, sauntering off. 'Only met him a handful of times. The man's a mystery.'

Jamie spots the man in lederhosen again. 'Who's that?' he asks.

Gracie grins. 'He's single, if that's what you're asking.'

'He was laughing at one of Matthew's stories,' Jamie says. 'But when I introduced myself as Matthew's friend, he just blanked me. It's happened a lot lately.'

Gracie lets out a loud giggle. 'Darling, I don't expect it's *you* they're snubbing.' She touches him affectionately on the cheek. 'You don't like Matthew?'

She plucks a glass of cheap fizz from a tray and leans in to Jamie. 'Don't take this the wrong way because I'm sure you know him better than anyone—it's simply that he's just *appeared*. No-one seems to know who the fuck he is.'

Gracie links arms with Jamie and strolls him, in a motherly fashion, around the room. There's a long story about her meeting David. 'He made all the costumes I wore while my band were touring South America. Never known anyone so talented. I've seen him take a piece of tin foil and turn it into a Russian space suit. Total magician.'

'Why South America?'

'Why not? Growing economies—seriously, *here* nobody knows who the fuck I am. *Peru*—I'm like Madonna.' She rubs him on the arm. 'So, you're a student?'

'I just finished my degree.'

'So you're looking for work?'

'I want to write.'

'So you're looking for work.' Gracie smiles.

'I am working.'

'As a writer?'

He lowers his head, shyly, avoiding Gracie's eyes now. No one seems to have noticed his uniform yet. Perhaps his attire stands out so much, they think he's selected it deliberately as a statement. 'I work at the *Scan 'n' Pack*.'

She squeezes his upper arm. 'Never mind darling—you can

write about what goes on in the locker room.'

Then she's distracted by someone on the other side of the room. 'Nice tats.'

Jamie squints. It's that guy again. Simon.

'I'm looking for someone with a great ass. He'd be perfect.'

'What for?' Jamie asks.

'Darling, I direct porn.'

'Porn?' Jamie can't help sounding surprised.

'Keeping the wolves from the door.' She peers at him from beneath her fringe. 'Maybe I could give *you* some work. Twink like you—made for it.'

Jamie giggles shyly.

'Don't knock it 'til you've tried it.' Gracie tells him about the other members of her crowd—a mixed bag of creatives and strays—none of whom had ever held down what Jamie's mother would call a 'proper job' or paid any tax. 'Marcel over there—' She points. 'He's a club promoter. Richard designs film-posters. Jeremy is a rent-boy and...'

'And Matthew?'

'I don't know about him.' She drains her glass. 'I'm just going to have a word with tattoo-boy. Get yourself another drink and grab me in ten minutes. We'll talk about how you're going to break London.'

She snakes elegantly into the crowd. Jamie's attention is diverted by Matthew, standing close to a man sporting a beard and a baseball cap. Even from this distance, Jamie can hear his American drawl, agreeing enthusiastically with Matthew.

Matthew splits off. Jamie approaches him and asks, 'An old friend?'

Matthew falters. 'We only just met.'

'Oh. I thought I saw a connection there.'

'I've never even been to America,' Matthew says emphatically.

Then Billy is in front of Jamie, giving him a start. 'What did I tell you about turning up in your work clothes? For fuck's sake!' Billy smiles. He's wearing a loose denim jacket, and a vest Jamie bought him when he still had money—black cotton with a print of a bulldog across the chest. Jamie recognises a familiar feeling—knees like water, the rest of the room blurring. Billy leans towards him and kisses him on the lips. Jamie is just about to habitually scan the room for onlookers, but he checks himself and instead pulls Billy towards him.

'You forgot to get me on the guest list,' Billy says. 'I had to flutter my eyelashes at the doorman.'

'Shit. Sorry, I was supposed to ask Matthew.'

'You're so preoccupied these days.' And there it is, that distance again.

'He's been so encouraging...' Jamie tells him about the tarot reading that Matthew had given him, and their trip to the *Mind, Body and Spirit Centre*. Billy stiffens, the way Jamie's father had on the day of his arrival.

'How can I talk to you about him, if you're going to react every time?'

Billy sighs. 'Okay. Try me...'

They walk around the periphery of the crowd. 'Do you think

he's ill?'

Billy looks up at the panelled ceiling. 'Are you asking me if I think he's got AIDS?'

'Yes.'

'How the fuck should I know? You can't tell just by looking.'

'*Billy*, he's greener than Kermit the Frog. And there's something wrong with his eyes. They flicker from side to side.'

'Drugs can make you go a bit cross-eyed.'

'He's totally anti-drugs!' Jamie says. 'He doesn't even use surface cleaner. He wipes the kitchen down with half a lemon. You know, I can't work him out. He works just four mornings a week and—'

'How's he surviving? Maybe you're right. Maybe he's on some sort of sickness benefit. It wouldn't surprise me.'

'What do you mean?' Jamie stares indignantly.

'He's a charlatan.'

Fear rises up in him. What if he's making a terrible mistake? And there it is again, the voice of his *mother*. 'You're wrong!' Jamie says. He throws back his glass of fizz, burps and thrusts it at Billy. 'Here, hold that. I'm going to the toilet.'

'The ladies toilets are over there,' Billy says, pointing to the corner of the room.

'Sexist!' Entering a vintage deco space of duck-egg-blue porcelain that he's sure is the gents', he's surprised to see Gracie Sharp standing in front of the mirror. She's concealing something on the side of the basin with her purse.

Damn Billy. 'I'm sorry, I must have the wrong—'

'No no,' she says. 'You've got the right loo. There's a queue in the women's and the boys here won't make a fuss.' She smiles, fluffs in the antique mirror and moves her purse gently. Underneath is a credit card and four lines of white crystalline powder. Jamie feels a rush of adrenaline.

She pulls a business card out and scribbles on it with eyeliner. 'This is home... and this is work,' Gracie hands it to him. 'Call me. Whenever you like.' She rolls up a note, puts it to her left nostril and snorts a line from the porcelain surface. Then she presses a finger against her other nostril and sniffs back, sharply. Tilting her head back, she leans into the mirror, checking for residue and wipes the back of her credit card against her tongue.

When Gracie looks back at him, Jamie feels himself blush. She offers him the note. 'It's cocaine. You want to try?'

'Isn't it very bad for you?'

'Extremely,' she says and touches her top lip with the point of her tongue.

'But doesn't it kill people?' he asks. *Shut up, Mother! SHUT UP!*

Bending to finish another line, Gracie's voice is lower, graver, 'Listen sweetheart, if you want to stay ahead of the plot—you've got to get to know the enemy.'

§

'What the fuck have you got on?' Billy flicks his fag butt into the driveway.

Jamie looks down at his turquoise tie-dyed kaftan. 'You don't like it?'

Billy throws his eyes up. 'Another one of Matthew's hand-me-downs?' He barges past Jamie, into the hallway. 'Is he home?'

'We're alone.' Jamie closes the door behind him. 'I got a job today.'

'Really? Where?'

'Gracie pulled a few strings at the Walter's Gallery. I went this morning. They told me straight away.'

'The woman from the party? You've learnt to schmooze then.' Billy hugs Jamie tightly. 'Well done, Soft Lad. When do you start?'

'Not for a few months yet. And I'm brassic…'

'Well, at least it'll fill Gloria's cakehole.' Billy sniffs the air. 'Mmmmm.'

'It's Thai.' Jamie closes the front door behind him.

'Thai?' Billy's eyes suddenly flare wide. 'Is this wise?'

'I thought I'd try.' Jamie's been at it all day, trying to get it right. 'I know you'd probably prefer a burger.'

'I'm happy to trying anything when it comes to your cooking but I'm talking about this shit.' Billy points at Matthew's collection of gaudy religious icons. 'You wonder why I don't want to come and visit you.'

'Open your mind, Billy.'

'Don't give me that clap-trap. This is *me* you're talking to now.'

Jamie sighs. 'You're beginning to sound like my mother.'

Billy pulls at the fabric of Jamie's kaftan. 'Listen, Soft Lad. I don't give a shit about the dust, or the décor. But your mother has got a point about the rest.' He lets the fabric fall again. 'And if you think I'm going to the theatre with you dressed like that, you've got another thing coming.'

§

Jamie cradles his programme in one arm as he springs down the street towards home. It's been a wonderful night with Billy. The tickets were expensive but so worth it. He can't wait to tell Matthew all about it. Oh London. Oh world! Isn't it beautiful to be so part of everything…

'Helloooo,' he calls as he enters the house. The hallway is imbued with the smells that Matthew always calls juniper and patchouli but Jamie doesn't know which is which.

'I'm just in the bath,' Matthew calls. 'I'll be down forthwith.'

'Relax. Enjoy your bath,' Jamie says.

'How was the play?'

'Amazing.'

'And the boy?'

'Tucked up in bed now.'

Jamie walks into the living room. There's a pot of tea on the table next to a pile of papers. As Jamie pours tea into a china cup, he can't help noticing the letter on top:

RLP Solicitors
Dear Matthew Morris,

Our Client: Mr MJ Nkanti
Property: 86 Gillet Street, Willesden Green, NW10
Re: Outstanding Sum Due

We act on behalf of the landlord Mr Nkanti and enclose a notice
terminating your tenancy of the premises on 31.01.98. We require
payment of rent arrears in the sum of £30,750 failing which—

'You still haven't christened that bed then?'

Jamie turns to Matthew in the doorway—snake hips and slim
torso rising above his towel draped waist. 'Who's Mr Nkanti?'

§

'What do you mean, it's not really *his* house?' Gloria throws her
oven gloves across the kitchen work surface. 'Whose bleedin'
house is it?' she asks.

Her fingers loop anxiously around the telephone cable. He'd
better not spin her a tale. She'll see straight through him. Terrible liar. But if she pushes too much, she knows he'll withdraw
and she'll get nowhere. She's already the *meddling mother*, slated
by *that thing*.

Jamie's voice is distant on the other end of the line as he tells
her how Matthew has lived in this house for over a decade even

though he's not the landlord. Her fingers move to her neck, scratching skin, already sore with anger. Initially, a guy in Africa owned it and a property management company collected the rent. Then Mr Nkanti moved back to England and came once a month to collect his money. One summer, he just stopped visiting. Matthew later found out that he'd died. Didn't leave a will. The estate went to probate. There was no one else to pay the rent to. And that was that. Until the letters started arriving.

A likely bloody story. 'So it's a squat. I knew it.'

'I wish you'd—' Jamie's voice is trembling.

'And what's been happening to all the money?'

'He's been saving it to give to the landlord. Why do you always have to think the worst?'

'Because I'm the one who picks up the pieces. He's not being honest with you, Jamie. He's not at all who you think he is. He barely works. Just some tuppenny-ha'penny job in a bloody bakery. He's constantly travelling. And you're just—'

'What's your aversion to me spreading my wings? Have you never felt like just running away—to live in different places, meet different people?'

She casts her mind back. People like her just didn't do that. At nineteen, she got a job as a telephonist, met Roy and got married. They worked to save for a deposit on a mortgage and before long she was expecting. 'Never had the opportunity, Jamie.' She sighs. 'Well, that's a lie. When your dad pisses me off, of course, I could run for the hills.'

'What about the swinging sixties, when everyone was taking

drugs and ripping their clothes off? Did you never feel like joining in?'

'No, love. That never happened in Welston.'

'Mum, can't you just learn to trust the universe…'

'That bloody vampire must have seen you coming, you soft sod.' She knows she shouldn't be speaking to him like this—like a child. She wants to leave it at that but she can't. 'So what's going to happen now?'

§

'America?' Jamie blurts, quickening his pace to keep up with Matthew.

'I know, I know. It's unfair. Especially as we've only just become friends.' Matthew's flapping his hands with excitement, walking heroically towards the funfair—a whirling light of red and yellow mathematical roulette curves and strobe.

Jamie stammers. 'How long are you going for?'

'I'm not sure. Who knows? I might like it so much I—'

'But you've only just met him! At the Gilbert and George exhibition.' Jamie can feel the floor of his stomach dropping from beneath him.

'Oh Jamie, there's the voice of your mother again. I thought you were going to put a stop to that? This is an amazing opportunity for me. And just think… you could come visit.'

'What if the Nkantis come back?' he says, voice rising above the generators and the din of a power-ballad issuing from the waltzers.

'We've been through this,' Matthew says. 'The house will be repossessed at some point but I have certain rights as sitting tenant. Don't worry about it. You'll have the place to yourself.'

Jamie's throat constricts. 'What about the convention we were going to go to?' His words come out high pitched and strangulated. 'The New-Age thing?'

'I know. I'm sorry.' Matthew's voice a tone of robotic mercilessness. 'You can take Billy instead.'

'How can you just drop everything and jet off in three days time to *Boulder, Colorado* or wherever it is? You've only known the man a matter of weeks.'

'There's no need to get upset, Jamie.'

'I'm not.'

'Clearly you are. His name is Dale. I met him in the Crêperie actually, where I met you. I knew as soon as I saw him that he was beautiful and kind and loving.' There's an impatient edge to his voice that makes Jamie retreat inwardly. 'He's really into crystal therapy—something I want to learn about. Jamie, it just feels right. The universe has offered this to me. I have to go.'

'Well I'm not trying to stop you.' Jamie can't look at him.

Matthew stops, grabs him by the shoulders. 'Jamie, what's really bothering you? It's not like we're in a relationship or anything. You've got Billy.' They've reached the middle of the park now. Families walk past them towards the fair.

'I'm being selfish.' Jamie offers after a tense silence.

'I'm sure you're not.' Matthew makes tight fists.

'It's just that…' Jamie looks down at Matthew's neon green socks peeping above suede hiking boots, even though it's nearly October. Even in this light, Jamie can see his gangly, hairless legs are covered with scratches from his rose bushes. He wonders just who is going to tend the garden. 'It's just that I've always dreamed of going to America.'

Matthew's fists open. 'Oh, fuck. Give me a hug.'

Relieved by this release of tension, Jamie flings his arms around him.

'You're going to love it,' Matthew laughs.

'Love what?'

'The USA.'

Jamie pulls away. 'I thought you'd never been?'

Matthew is stunned. 'I haven't,' he says eventually.

'Then how do you know I would love it?'

'I just do.' Matthew pulls Jamie to him again and kisses him on the lips. 'Pull yourself together. I feel like a spin on the waltzers.'

In a carriage on his own, legs spread, locking himself into position, Matthew rides the waltzers three times in a row. He throws his head back and laughs wickedly. Jamie feels sick just to watch.

'You must spin,' Matthew says, stepping off the ride. 'Every day. It helps to make the chakras spin faster, allowing you to interpret and process information faster. Why don't you come on with me?'

'I can't.'

'Why?'

'I'm scared.'

'Trust the universe, Jamie.'

§

Jamie is listening to the music of Philip Glass. Every time he hears that music, it connects him to Matthew. Since he's been away the house has felt so empty. There's been no exotic food or smells. There are no magical conversations about the mysteries of the universe. Life is just a bit dull.

But—no uniform, no checkout—Jamie's booked a week off from work to do *nice* things. He can be like Matthew—hanging out in coffee shops with a notepad, going to the cinema during the *daytime* while it's quieter and cheaper. And ordering takeaway Thai meals.

When the doorbell rings, Jamie checks his appearance in the hallway mirror and opens the door. He was expecting a delivery man on the doorstep, but instead a tall, smartly-suited and dark-skinned black man, carrying a London A-Z, stands sideways to him on the doorstep.

'Hello.' Jamie smiles widely, yet regrets opening the door—*bloody double-glazing salesmen.*

'I'm looking for Matthew Morris,' the man says.

'I'm sorry. He's not here right now. Can I help?' Jamie folds his arms across his pounding chest.

'I'm Mr Nkanti. I am the owner of this house.'

§

'The desert? You? Oh, Jamie you're not going to last two minutes out there. You're just so...'

'Green?' Jamie replies.

'I was going to say *homely*. A nester.'

'You think I'm not capable.'

'I don't think you should go.' Billy shakes his head. He's wearing the same blue denim baseball cap that he'd been wearing when they first met. 'How can you trust him, after all this business with the so called Mr Nkanti?'

Jamie sighs. 'I've got to give him the benefit of the doubt. Has it occurred to you that maybe he wasn't lying? Maybe the owner of the house did die and the Mr Nkanti who turned up at the house was his son or, I don't know, his brother.'

'Maybe. But you don't know for sure, do you, Jamie.'

'Well, where else am I going to go? The job at the gallery doesn't start for another few months.'

'Well, you could—'

'I can't stand another *day* with mum and dad, and if I move in with you... Well, you've said it yourself, we'll be tripping over each other in this little room.'

'Jamie, just think about it.'

Jamie looks away. He'll show Billy. 'I have thought about it. You know how much I've always wanted to visit America. Here's my chance. I can go and stay with Matthew. He says it won't cost me a thing. This must be the universe speaking.'

Billy sighs deeply. 'The money is the least of your worries. One sign of a spider and—'

'Watch me. I'm going on this trip. I'll be a different man when I come home.'

§

Wispy threads of silver swirl across a cerulean sky streaked with rose and violet and bright, blinding tangerine. The setting sun reflects off the bonnet of Dale's jeep like a laser, as they pull onto the ridge of Sandia Crest. A halo in front of them is dramatic enough to inspire an almost religious experience in Jamie.

He clutches his copy of *The Prophetic Insights*, the one personal item he didn't leave at Billy's place after the eviction. A photograph of Billy, standing in for a bookmark, is sticking out of the pages. Jamie touches Billy's youthful face with a fingertip. Did they need this much space?

'This is only the beginning,' Matthew says, his mood, perhaps, warming after his strange behaviour at the airport.

'Incredible,' Jamie whispers, unsure if it's Matthew's conduct or the altitude that is unsettling him.

'I wanted you to see this,' Matthew says, now with childlike candour.

As they drive on in silence, above the twinkling lights of Albuquerque and beyond—the meandering snow-capped mountains, Jamie ruminates. They do things differently here. Only an hour ago he'd been on the connecting flight from Houston, Texas to Albuquerque, New Mexico. His first ever long-haul journey had been fucking turbulent. As soon as he'd set foot on American soil, he'd been greeted by stern airport staff, who had been military in their handling of passengers. He'd rushed from one side of the airport to the other to check-in his bags for the connecting flight.

Matthew and Dale met him at the airport in Albuquerque, as arranged. Something was different in Matthew. Perhaps the two of them, Dale and Matthew, had quarrelled prior to his arrival.

'One thing, Jamie,' Matthew said, quite sharply, before Jamie could even set his rucksack down on the tarmac. 'We've used a hell of a lot of diesel getting here and it costs such a lot. We wondered if you would fill the tank up.'

There was absolutely no question of Jamie not paying his way but he hadn't factored in the cost of diesel. On the phone, Matthew had been emphatic about the trip not costing him anything.

'October will be a fantastic time,' Matthew had said. 'It'll be just nearing the end of summer and the *light*—Jamie, the sky goes on forever. You must come for at least a month. It'll still be warm.'

'But you're in the middle of the desert —' Jamie had offered.

'Let the universe take care of everything.' Matthew had said.

Okay, there were a few hundred pounds in his account, saved from his extra shifts at the *Scan'n'Pack*, to get him through the next few months. There was also an overdraft, set up in case of emergencies. But... 'But I only have enough for the airfare. Catching a bus—'

'Dale has money. We'll collect you in the jeep.'

The implication was that they'd changed their minds and he was now just a great inconvenience to them. Realising the cost of filling up that jeep might be all he had in his wallet, Jamie shifted his weight, nervously, from one leg to the other.

He had observed, with some confusion, that Dale seemed a friendly enough person. The blackest of moustaches only served to embellish an already good-natured mouth, through which he'd cheered, 'Heard so much about you.' He carried Jamie's bags to the jeep and offered him water to drink. Matthew, on the other hand, had seemed to be enjoying Jamie's edginess.

'You should ride in the front. You'll get a better view. I don't want you to miss a thing,' Matthew said. 'It's a long drive to Taos, especially at night. So we thought we'd make a stop off, if that's alright—a couple of friends. Tomorrow we'll take the Turquoise Trail, as it's commonly known. We'll be in Taos by tomorrow evening. Take lots of photographs.'

'Yeah, whatever, that's fine,' Jamie said. 'I'm easy.'

'It's just that Dale had to drive all the way here, nearly a day and a half travelling, and it's really not fair for him to have to drive back right now.'

'Oh, I should have brought my driving licence,' Jamie said.

'Don't say "should" Jamie,' Matthew said. 'It implies a sense of guilt. I "could", but I didn't. You see, it's not the same thing at all.'

Matthew was so direct. Jamie wanted to believe he was

teasing, but it felt like an accusation. He breathed out. 'No, all I meant was—'

'Well, maybe it would have been better for you to have caught a Greyhound,' Dale said.

Now, as they drive from the dark airport, the sky gradually turns lighter as they rise higher up into the mountains, racing towards a disappearing sun. Albuquerque glistens, an emerald city beneath them. On the dark road, the yellow markings curve underneath the jeep as they ascend a serpent of sheer hairpins into the distant Sandia Mountains.

'Pale and Gegger—they're not a couple,' Matthew asserts. 'They live in Gegger's Grandmother's old shack. You're going to really like them.'

Jamie fiddles with his seatbelt. It's all happening so fast. Jet-lag? Altitude sickness? Jamie can't read the situation at all. Maybe he just needs some sleep. 'Are you sure it's alright? I mean, turning up with a complete stranger.'

'Gegger said it would be fine, whenever we were passing.'

§

It's *Pumpkin Season* in New Mexico. With his weighty rucksack leaning against his ankles, Jamie views the front of a duck-egg-blue shack, glowing with pumpkin lanterns in preparation for Halloween. It's reminiscent of a gingerbread house in an illustrated version of Hänsel und Gretel. Rows of dried chilli-peppers hang from the eves of the shack, an ancient pueblo custom, according to Matthew.

Night has closed in. Except for the brilliance of the pumpkin lanterns, it's difficult to see. Jamie wonders who could be bothered to light so many candles, out here in the middle of nowhere—such a time-consuming and whimsical thing to do, yet beautiful in effect.

The air is filled with the clicking and popping of insects. A willowy, squinting figure makes its way from the shack, through a hinged bug screen, carrying out trash. Jamie takes the figure for a female in this light: long blonde hair tied back, a lacy, blousy shirt, loose fitting trousers and flip-flops. As his eyes grow accustomed to the darkness, he can see the figure is actually male. The screen slaps shut behind him. He dumps the rubbish, and walks down the small steps towards the jeep.

'Pale,' Matthew calls in a slithery public-relations intonation that Jamie has become familiar with. 'Hi.'

'Hey.' This mono-syllable, in contrast, is not altogether friendly. 'Now what in tarnations do we have here?' Jamie watches Pale's face as they make their *hellos*. It's smooth and elegant and finely boned, as if carved from ivory. Lines like Russian filigree have been hand-tattooed around his lips. He wears eyeliner around deep-set eyes and his long witchlike fingers are tipped with black nail varnish.

'And you must be Jamie,' he starts, in a comparatively kinder manner. 'Look at this. Is this the 1940s?' he says, pointing to Jamie's clothes.

'Original.' Jamie grins, begining to warm to him. He's wearing a vintage Bretton sailor jumper and pair of bell-bottoms, a rather eccentric get up for Houston airport. The outfit had turned a few heads—not in a good way.

'You look fantastic,' he says. 'Let's get inside before the grizzlies come and get you. Gegger has just put the kettle on.'

'Bears?' Jamie says, shuddering.

'If *they* don't get you, the snakes and spiders will.'

'*Spiders?*'

'Tarantulas.'

Jamie lifts his arms into the air and looks around his feet.

'Don't worry.' The man laughs, registering his fear. 'All the spiders will be hibernating now. Too cold for them. Snakes too.' He steps forward and takes Jamie's rucksack. 'I'm Pale.'

Jamie's reticence falls away inside the shack. It resembles a grotto, adorned to excess. Every surface is covered with spooky paraphernalia—skulls, voodoo dolls, incense burners, dreamcatchers, masks. Old Indian curios are collected on top of shelves and dressers. There are candles everywhere and the walls are lined with shelves of books about witchcraft and UFOs. A mannequin standing in the corner is made up to look like Jane Mansfield.

'You like?' Pale asks.

'Oh yeah,' Jamie says. What strikes him most are the paintings that cover the wall surrounding a small fireplace.

'They're mine.' Pale says. Matthew and Dale have been forgotten, still standing in the doorway. 'Come in, guys, and take a seat.'

They walk in and sit on couches covered in old Indian woven rugs.

'They're beautiful,' Jamie says, staring at the brutal images. Each one seems to be a portrait of a child with a mature adult face, painted with impossibly smooth brush strokes, wearing decorative smocks and suits, like Victorian cameos. Jamie wonders if they are therapy for Pale—a seepage of exquisite pain and oil on canvas. The paintings make him feel grounded again.

'I'm looking to have a show in LA. And maybe later in London,' Pale says.

Another man enters from the kitchen. 'Hello, Jamie,' he says. His unkempt bespectacled face is reminiscent of a young Allen Ginsberg. 'I'm Gegger.' His voice is an aristocratic Vincent Price-like drawl.

After their introductions, Gegger hands Jamie a cup of steaming liquid. 'Green tea. It should help with the fatigue after the distance you've travelled.'

'A fantastic home you have,' Jamie says, admiring the shack.

Dale has made himself comfortable on one of two Arabian style divans, fiddling playfully with his facial hair. Pale seats himself on the opposite divan and pats the space next to him, rearranging cushions and a crocheted blanket to make room for Jamie.

Pale and Gegger amuse Jamie with stories of their past. Pale had been a go-go dancer in various nightclubs—first in San Francisco and later in Los Angeles. The sincerity about his personal life makes Jamie comfortable, even though the subject matter is intimate.

'I started doing porn during my mid-twenties. Easy money. But the filmmakers—they were pretty narrow-minded. They obviously had a certain role in mind, because of my build, and the way I look. I always ended up being the bottom.'

'That must have been pretty demanding.' Two days before, Jamie hadn't expected to find himself talking about the precise details of a sex worker's life but here they are.

'It's difficult to get fucked when you're not aroused. So I took drugs.'

'What kind of drugs?' Jamie imagines a scene in his head: Pale, ass in the air before a shaky camera, surrounded by a camera crew, while having to appear relaxed and desirable for the viewer.

'I got hooked on Tina—crystal meth.'

He'd heard of whole towns in the US that had been ripped apart by this substance. 'It keeps you up for days and you can fuck forever on it.'

Matthew is sucking the inside of his cheek between his teeth, his motif of disapproval. He gets up and walks to the bathroom.

Gegger makes more tea while Pale tells the rest of his story— of moving away from the city to rebuild his life. Gegger, also a recovering addict, from time to time falls off the wagon. 'Pale, darling, I think it might be time for my heroin.'

It was good judgement not to have taken Gracie up on her offer of a career in porn. He admires Pale for his frankness and strength of character—a man whose stories resonate with authenticity. Clearly, Pale's recovery from crystal meth abuse fuels his paintings. Jamie wonders how long it will be before this destructive white powder reaches the streets of Soho. Then he overhears Matthew and Gegger in the kitchen. 'Actually, Jamie hasn't eaten since he got off the plane. Would it be alright to cook something?'

Jamie registers a look of *He's got a nerve!* on Gegger's face.

'If you'd given me more notice,' Pale says. 'I would have prepared something earlier. When you called, I assumed you just—'

'I can do it,' Matthew says. 'I'm at home in anyone's kitchen. Do you have any vegetables? Garlic?'

Jamie leaps up, detecting an obvious animosity between them both. 'I hope you're not going to any trouble on my account.'

Pale touches him on the arm. 'It's fine, honey. You just relax.'

An hour later, they are surrounded by food. 'This is lovely,' Jamie says, looking at the table—cups of wine, bread, soup, green vegetables. 'It's so good of you to do this, Gegger.'

'Thank Matthew. *He* did all the cooking.'

'But I mean to put us up, like this, at short notice.' Jamie locks eyes with Gegger.

'It's fine, our pleasure.' Gegger smiles, reassuringly.

'So, New Mexico?' Jamie asks, shovelling food into his mouth.

'This is the home of Roswell. The infamous airbase where a UFO crash-landed in the 40s. The government allegedly quarantined beings from outer space here.'

'Do you believe all the stories?' Jamie asks.

'If I were to believe all those stories, I really would go mad,'

Gegger says. 'New Mexico does have its fair share of crackpots.'

Pale nods. 'Weird tales are official currency in New Mexico.'

Matthew latches onto Jamie's enthusiasm. 'When I was much younger,' he says. 'I went to visit a friend in Cornwall. South of England, Gegger.'

'King Arthur territory.' Gegger sips wine.

'That's right. I was staying in a large house. I was in a room on one side of the building away from everyone else.' Matthew's eyes sparkle; he seemingly loves the attention. Jamie leans closer. 'On the third night, I woke up in bed, sensing something in the room. I'd been sleeping on my own, of course. I was startled. I tried to move to get up. I was fixed. Paralyzed.'

'Were you actually awake?' Pale asks.

'I felt a gentle pressure on the side of my legs, which moved to my thighs.'

'Did you scream?' Pale giggles.

Matthew continues in earnest. 'I couldn't move my lips. The more I tried to move, the more helpless I became. My eyes became accustomed to the light. A thin black figure was leaning over me, face hidden. I knew it wasn't human.'

Here we go again, Jamie thinks.

'I felt it move its hand to my crotch.'

'Oh, brother.' Pale stands and starts collecting plates.

'I was determined not to let this continue. I forced the sound out of my body and shouted a firm 'No!' And then it just faded away.'

'And you say New Mexico is bad.' Jamie looks in Gegger's

direction.

Gegger exchanges a look with Pale who's moving behind Matthew with the plates.

After Jamie finishes the washing up, they all settle in the cosy living area. 'Jamie, you know, it's a real pleasure to have you here,' Pale says, in earnest. Jamie feels such joy for having met them both. Yet he senses Matthew isn't so smitten with the idea of them all getting on.

Gegger asks him about his writing and Jamie takes the opportunity to tell him about a collection of stories he's written.

'You didn't tell me you'd published a book,' Matthew says, blankly.

'I wrote three. They were rejected,' Jamie says.

Out of Matthew's deadpan face seeps spiteful satisfaction.

'Three books! It's those who keep going who make it in the end,' Pale says. 'Don't give up. Rise above the competition.'

'We'll get up early and drive along the *Turquoise Trail.*' Matthew says. 'Stopping off at Madrid, Cerrillos and Santa Fe. You'll be amazed by the sights, Jamie. Then we'll head to Taos and the desert where our dome is.'

'Gosh. You live all the way out there, do you?' Gegger asks.

'Taos is to the New-Age movement as Mecca is to Islam.' Pale says, emphatically. 'There are no children in the town. It's full of transients, nomads and orphans. No-one actually grows up there.'

'The day after tomorrow, we'll be getting ready for the party,' Matthew says.

'Party?' Jamie blushes nervously.

'In *your* honour. It's going to be just wonderful.'

'Swell,' Pale says, an odd look passing across his face.

'It'll be Jamie's initiation to things,' Matthew adds.

Initiation. The hairs on the back of Jamie's neck stand on end.

'You'll be coming, of course?' Dale asks.

Gegger looks at Pale.

'You must,' Matthew says, placing a bony hand on Jamie's shoulder.

A corner of Pale's mouth curls up. 'Yes. We'll come.'

'You don't have to come on my account,' Jamie says. 'It's so far!' Drive across the desert? To go to a party? It's inconceivable to him.

Gegger tilts his head at Jamie, a look signalling something between alliance and fatherly reassurance. 'We can't let this be the last time we see you, Jamie. And a party in Taos desert— who could stay away?'

§

Shaken from sleep, Jamie feels Matthew's fingers probing his ribs.

'We have to go *now*, if you're going to catch it,' Matthew whispers.

'Catch what?' Jamie moans and pulls sheets up over his shoulders.

'The sunrise from Sandia Crest.' Matthew looks at him in

astonishment, as if he'd committed an act of blasphemy.

Jamie's so tired his eyes roll back inside his head. 'What time is it?'

'Five-thirty.'

§

The rising golden disc behind translucent cotton wool clouds makes the sky look as if it is on fire. From an aesthetic point of view, no one can argue that it's not spectacular but Jamie has never really understood the symbolism that people attach to sunrises. They're a bit like New Year's Eve; expectation unreached. He casts his mind back to the last one he'd seen. He must have been about fourteen. He, Gloria and Roy had sat looking at the golden fire above the ocean from the coastland of the Gower Peninsula. A week before, at school, he'd been beaten, badly: the usual thugs. From the beginning of that holiday, he'd been afraid to take his shirt off on the beach, ashamed of the bruises, fearing that he would expose who, no, *what* he was. There are darknesses that no amount of sunlight can take away.

Sitting next to Matthew on a rock at Sandia Crest, the sun has started to spill onto the buildings out in front of him, vast swathes of golden light seeping out of the mothership.

'Just look at it. A new day,' Matthew says. And then he turns to Jamie. 'A new life.'

§

Miles of open road stretch out in front of them, punctuated now and then by old colonial church buildings, disused gas stations and telegraph poles. Desert plains turn incongruously into mountain ranges low on the horizon as the lone jeep cruises languidly along the tarmac. The sun, at its zenith, creates no shadows on an alien landscape that seems to beat and breathe as if it is alive.

They stop off, firstly at Madrid, a mining town, almost exclusively populated by lesbians, then spend a few hours in the state's artistic capital, Santa Fe, where they load up the back of the jeep with pumpkins. It seems Matthew wants so much for him to like all of this. Dale had been so kind in fetching him from the airport. It would be ungrateful and ridiculous to whine about homesickness. He misses the concrete reassurances of Billy. He'd do anything for one of his hugs. And any talk of London lowers the temperature and triggers a change of subject. Matthew points to the decorative dried chillies on the eaves of the buildings and collections of pots. 'This is traditional Indian pueblo work.'

In the afternoon they set off for Taos. The jeep roars down through sagebrush desert. Jamie feels the wind tickle his hair. He's connected to something primal as they move over one more ridge and toward the Sangre de Christo Mountains ascending before them.

'It's so different here. Sometimes I feel I'm on another planet,' Matthew says. 'The people are extraordinary. Everyone has some sort of quirk. Prunella Small—'

'Author of *The Prophetic Insights*?'

'Yes, I've been doing some housekeeping for her.'

Jamie twists to look behind at Matthew. 'You're kidding?'

'She has this healing machine, invented by a Russian scientist.' Matthew's voice is flat, as if talking about something banal like having forgotten to empty the laundry basket. 'It works by analysing a person's aura and presenting the results visually.'

Jamie reaches into this rucksack for a pad and pen. Glimpses of character and dialogue like this will surely make it into a book he writes one day.

'Aurographs are a bit old hat, Matthew, no?'

'It's not an aurograph. *This* is interactive. Let's say for instance, you have bowel cancer—just hypothetically. The defective energy pattern would show on the machine.'

Jamie nods.

'They use the machine to project energy into the affected area. Thus making you well again. It's revolutionary.'

'Sounds rather Frankensteinian to me.'

'Listen, it could help people with all sorts of cancers. It could help people with HIV and AIDS. And they have it here, right in the middle of New Mexico.'

'So how come they're not using this technology in England, on the NHS.'

'Only just scratched the surface,' Matthew says.

Jamie looks at Matthew's sickly pallor and hasn't got the nerve to ask if this is why he came here. 'Suppose it got into the wrong hands. Too much energy in the wrong areas. You could really fuck someone up.'

'Exactly. She's had her fair share of detractors.'

The Taos desert fills his vision like the sound of an organ filling an empty church.

Matthew points to a tiny speck in front of them. 'See the groove? That's the Rio Grande. See the tiny dot in the desert about a mile above it?'

'Yes.'

'That's the dome.'

'Incredible, isn't it?' Dale says. 'Home.'

The setting sun bathes everything in a final warm glow, as they pull up outside the dome. It then falls behind the mountains, and an immense shadow flies towards them, covering the surface of the desert, as swift as a bed sheet being drawn across a mattress.

Speechless, Jamie steps from the vehicle and almost loses his footing, as he makes contact with Taos soil.

'We rented it from an architect,' Dale says.

The geodesic dome, constructed entirely of tessellated triangles, is set in the desert like a crash-landed spaceship. The living quarters, it would appear, are partially above and below ground. There's a fresh-water tank to one side of the dome and large solar panel. The smell of shit, floating in a barrel of chemical is masked, only partially, by a small herb garden and fruit trees.

Matthew sets about lighting a fire inside a ring of stones. Inside the dome is decorated with bright colours and Mexican patterned textiles, which remind Jamie of retreats he's read about in books. 'It's like a hippy commune,' Jamie jokes.

Dale shows Jamie to the loft that will be his sleeping area, in the upper hemisphere of the dome. 'The walls are plastered adobe style to keep the room cool during the summer and warm in the winter.'

Jamie changes into jeans and a fleece before joining them beside Matthew's fire. It crackles and pops. Dry rocks, packed with air trapped inside them, explode spectacularly, sending Matthew wild with childlike joy. He turns around on the spot, beginning his spinning routine. The fire draws up dry leaves and dust, the way fire does, sending a blizzard of burning snowflakes falling upwards.

'Does it get cold like this every night?' Jamie says.

'Yes,' Dale says. 'I think it may snow, very soon.'

Matthew stops revolving.

'Snow?' Hadn't Matthew said the weather would be warm? Jamie's hardly prepared for winter. Matthew turns away. Jamie feels like he's been set up. He clenches his teeth together, thinking about two months here in the cold.

In the distance, there are a few caravans, a couple of earthships and a stockade surrounding a large motorhome. Further away, highlighted by the last strip of orange sunlight, Taos glistens like a spillage of caster sugar on a kitchen work surface. This is the only other sign of real civilization for miles and separating Jamie from it, the valley of the Rio Grande.

'How long does it take to get to Taos centre from here, Dale?'

'About forty-five minutes.'

'Walk?'

'No. Drive. You couldn't walk, really. There's only one bridge across the ravine and that's over there,' Dale says, pointing blindly into the expanse, which is now mostly in shadow. 'I suppose you could hitch-hike. But it's fine, you'll come with us, in the jeep.'

Jamie squints at the sprinkling of golden sugar. Dale points to the snow-capped Sangre de Christo Mountains. 'That's a ski-resort, at this time of year.'

'What's behind the mountains?' Jamie asks.

'Colorado,' Dale says.

'And beyond that?'

'Utah.'

Jamie processes a thought. He looks across the landscape at Taos, and the thought emerges.

Snow.

§

A chill nip wakes Jamie. Through a little window in the domed loft he can see a panorama, as if sprinkled with desiccated coconut, interrupted occasionally by the skeletal branches of sagebrush and a baleen of aspens bristling at the edge of the forest.

The many thousands of miles travelled have left an impression on Jamie's aching body. Matthew and Dale are already up, making breakfast, listening to the weather report. He struggles to lift himself off the bed. 'Morning all.'

They watch what can only be described as *limited news*—something about homeless pets in Albuquerque, a mystery shooting in Roswell, 120 Elk found dead near to a crop circle, while Matthew serves omelettes. There's nothing about Britain, London, the rest of the world.

'We're lucky if we hear anything about the rest of America, let alone the UK. It's how they control us,' Dale says, from the round sofa in the circular living area.

'They like to keep people impaired.' Matthew turns off the TV in protest.

All day they prepare for the party. Jamie collects firewood. Matthew spends hours cooking and Dale carves hideous faces in the pumpkins they transported from Santa Fe.

'It's going to be just wonderful,' Matthew says.

But who will come? Apart from the odd caravan plot and the four or five nearby earth-ships, there are no neighbouring desert inhabitants. Not enough guests for a knitting circle, let alone a *party*.

'They'll come,' Matthew says. 'Believe me.'

At eight o'clock, Jamie stands before the large picture window, as the sun creeps down an orange and purple sweet-wrapper sky. A faint sketch of road, crosses the Rio Grande, picked out by a fine trail of car head-lamps twinkling like fairy lights. 'Look at that,' Jamie says. He feels a sense of dread, as if about to go on stage in front of thousands to sing a song to which he does not know the words.

'The guests,' Matthew squeals.

'There must be forty or fifty vehicles in convoy,' Jamie says, pointing and counting. 'Who would cross a desert for someone they never met?'

'I told you it's going to be special.'

Twenty minutes later, the three of them are outside smelling the creosote bushes still wet from frost and the smoke from a beacon of fire lit earlier by Dale. A lady in a turquoise jogging-suit springs out of a rusty old car. The car cannot be hers, *surely*. He knows she's got money to burn, with that book selling out worldwide.

'Prunella!' Matthew shrieks, performing a sycophantic pan-tomime of bending and flapping. 'You made it!'

'Mercury might be in retrograde but of course I made it,' she says. 'What did you expect—that we'd miss the turning and plummet into the Rio Grande? I brought my faithful driver with me.' A portly man climbs out of the driver's side. He looks like he's going woodcutting rather than to a party. Matthew had sketched in the details earlier: local sheriff, always 'on duty'. Though what sort of heinous crime could occur here in the de-sert, Jamie couldn't guess.

'Steve!' Matthew cries, as if they are long lost relatives.

Prunella might be anything from fifty-five to seventy-five years old; it's impossible to place her age. Her face, framed by a helmet of curly white hair, is hidden behind large turquoise sunglasses. She's tiny next to Matthew, not at all like the image Jamie had in his head. Flinging her arms wide, a bottle in each hand, she greets Matthew with a hug. He has to stoop. *Inside,* he beckons, *come, come.*

As they move inside, Matthew introduces Jamie to Prunella. Tiny as she is, she's also a gushy and expansive *let's talk about me* sort of character. *Look at me—my aura is clean. I can turn lead into gold. You too can be like me. I even wrote a book about it. Positivity is the key. Banish negativity. Out! Out! Out! Open your heart to the universe. Behold the new era. Let the vibration of light penetrate you. See it. Create it. Grasp it. The Universe will support you in your work.*

Jamie is mute. He'd always imagined meeting her. He would be vivacious and entertaining and she would find him charming. But no—he cannot find the words. He'd thought she might be more, well, friendly.

'Jamie,' she purrs, standing in the middle of the dome. 'It's so wonderful to have you here in Taos, after so long. Matthew tells me you're writing a book,' she says, with an affirming smile.

'Well, I have a few ideas but—'

'You wanna write a book—*write a book*! Put the energy out there and it will come back to you, tenfold.'

'Thank you. I'll give it a go,' he says, politely.

'Trust me, honey.'

'It's good to meet you,' he says, awkwardly.

'We've been waiting for your *return*, Jamie.'

What does she mean? There's no sense in challenging her. A question would only open up another can of spaghetti symbols. It might be easier just to go along with it all.

By half-past eight the dome is crowded with people. How

Matthew has got to know so many people in the short time he's been here, Jamie has no idea. There must be fifty or sixty people and more arriving all the time. Matthew hands Jamie a tray of food to take round, a task he exploits in order to meet everyone in the room. He can feel their Taos eyes upon him, working him out; even fingers pointing. That's *him. He's the one Matthew told us about.*

He bumps into a woman, swathed in purple crushed velvet. She's about fifty. *Dyed* hair. If she's prepared to use chemicals, then she can't be *that* New Age.

'I'm Bunni,' she says. 'Jamie, yes?'

Everyone in the room knows who he is but *he* doesn't know any of them.

'You're going to do great work here, with Matthew. I know it.'

'I'm sorry… *work?*'

'Well, I don't mean *work* work. You'll take to it easily.'

'I don't follow.'

'You're working on *The Book*, aren't you?'

'You mean, my writing.'

'I mean *The Book*.' She nods and smiles.

He inhales deeply. 'I'm working on *a* book.'

'You know, the light coming from your aura is extraordinary.'

A few months ago, he might have fallen for this. He'd have even convinced himself that he could see his aura—beautiful colours surrounding him like a halo. Matthew had once said he could read them—stare into the invisible light and say how someone was feeling or what kind of person they were.

'Same colour as Matthew's,' Bunni says. 'Well, it would be, wouldn't it?'

'Why? Jamie fixes a smile and forms his eyes into a question. 'You being *brothers*.'

'Is that what he told you—that we're brothers?' He hears his voice slide high, as he looks over at the kitchen—Matthew slicing lemons, mixing some concoction with herbs in it.

Bunni's arm, strangled from wrist to elbow with bangles, reaches out and clutches him. Jamie looks at the hand squeezing his arm, aiming, possibly, to reassure, until it retreats again, fingers sparkling with clusters of opals. 'I know you're not siblings in your *human* form. Perhaps you've blocked it out.'

'I'm not blocking anything,' he assures her, stiffly folding his arms.

'This is the site, where you landed. From the Hermetes.'

'Hermetes?' Now he feels a violent urge to bite her.

'A star constellation, on the other side of our sun.'

'Look, I didn't. I'm from the UK. From bloody Welston.'

'Still holding onto personal information that you've learned to carry. Usually, folk have worked through this by now. Don't worry. We'll help you prepare.'

They've got him entirely wrong. He's partly incredulous, partly—

'Listen to me.' She leans into him. 'You and Matthew were separated and now you're reunited, at last, to do great work here in Taos.'

Jamie has brought himself to this place. So many unanswered

questions about the universe—now he wishes he'd never asked. Obviously, extra-terrestrials exist but to suggest that *he* is one of them—no, that's going off the script. If only he'd listened to his mother. Sceptical and scared of taking risks she might be, but she is at least a good judge of character. It is all rather *Emperor's New Clothes*. What should he do now? Pretend that he can actually see the finest silk and blend in with the others, or—expose them for what they are?

Bunni is prattling on about them all being from the family of light and all this important work they have to do while they are in the physical plane.

'We are all emerging from denial,' she says. 'Even Prunella has found it hard. In fact, her own family have turned against her. She adored her grandson. They won't let her see him anymore. They think she's a bad influence. But she's committed to the project, so she accepts she has to let go.'

Jamie's chest tightens. Her mad glassy eyes drill into his as she burbles on and on about him needing to let go of the personal information that comforts him during his time on Earth. 'It anchors you to the physical realm and keeps you separate from the universal pool of wisdom—your family, your birthplace, your name. You must let it all go before you become non-physical again and return to the light.'

He hears no emotion or irony in her voice. 'After the initiation, a process to remove this information will commence.'

'Initiation?'

'I think it will make Matthew feel better when you return to the family. Must be a bit strange for you. Though I wouldn't say too much to the others about that. Resistance tends to cause negative vibrations.'

Across the room, Gegger and Pale have arrived. Pale's wearing a black cat-suit with a silver O-ring belt. His blonde hair, plaited and swirled up on his head, is more suited to a swanky art opening in New York City, than a glass dome in the sagebrush desert. Gegger looks gloomy in his beat blacks and his wayfarer half-framed glasses. Jamie grins in their direction, eager to catch their attention and escape Bunni. Matthew sweeps Pale and Gegger from him, across the room to the hexagonal couch near Prunella.

Bunni touches him on the elbow. He flinches and she withdraws, as if expecting him to hit her—her fat little fingers tipped with green nail varnish, remain hanging in the air.

'Matthew has been through a lot recently,' she says. 'He was almost abducted again, when the *others* came.'

'Abducted?'

Recovering now, she opens cigarette papers, preparing to roll. 'They're constantly fighting for occupancy of this land.'

'They should give it back to the Indians, if you ask me,' Jamie says, partially under his breath, trying to bring things back to reality.

Bunni looks across the room at a Native American Indian man. 'Shamboo, over there. He'll tell you about it. He was abducted too. It's not uncommon in these parts. And so was my son. And then we found out about you—'

'You've made a mistake. I've never been abduc—'

'It's the block again.' She puts the joint in her mouth and sparks up. 'The others—the dark ones are trying to deplete our resources. They want to see how we've evolved. That's why they perform the abductions.'

Jamie surveys the room. 'Bunni, I really must say hello to a few more people. Do you mind if I circle the room? We can continue later.'

She holds the joint up to him. 'Do you think they'll mind?'

He shakes his head. 'Matthew doesn't like smoke.'

'He's so pure, isn't he? Do you want some?'

He'd love to numb the evening away but he doesn't trust what might be inside the joint. 'No, thank you.'

He heads for Gegger and Pale. Matthew catches him by the elbow. 'Getting to know everyone?'

Jamie tries to look cheery. Pale and Gegger are chatting to Prunella Small, stunned looks on their faces.

'We're extremely lucky to be amongst such special people,' Matthew says. 'Come on, I want you to meet Steve. He's one of us.'

One of us? Fuck! They're all bonkers. Steve, ordinary as he looks, in his plaid shirt and Stetson, sounds eccentric to say the least. 'You're waking up from that trance state, Jamie,' Steve says. 'Try not to be sceptical. You are an artist. An artist's job is to tell the truth.' Jamie fiddles with his shirt cuffs, trying to avoid Steve's intensity. 'Think of the great artists and writers. Look at Orwell, Verne, Arthur C. Clarke. We are living in their future.

Do people need any further convincing? All will become clear after the initiation.'

Steve rambles on, turning now to Prunella, using words that Jamie struggles to catch the meaning of. Prunella rattles off soundbites from the self-help universe—about enlightened beings, a new world order. When the subject turns to some conspiracy at government level, Jamie is able to peel off and finally makes his way across the dome to Gegger and Pale.

'Jesus, am I glad to see you two.'

Their forced smiles can't disguise their alarm. 'What on Earth are you doing here?'

Jamie stares, unsure of the answer.

'You don't fit with these people,' Pale says. He leans in close and lowers his voice. 'These people are not your friends, Jamie. I knew from the moment I met you at our shack. You've been unfortunate to get mixed up with them.'

A mixture of fear and loyalty rises up in Jamie's stomach. 'Hang on a minute—Matthew is my friend.' He glances over at Matthew, who is raising his voice to Bunni in the open plan kitchen area. 'What's the problem? It's just a doobie,' he can hear her saying over the din of the party. Then Matthew is pouring some green liquid infused with herbs from a bottle and laughs spitefully at something with Prunella.

'You should hear the stuff they've been telling us,' Gegger says.

Jamie turns back to them, now less defensively. 'Thank God I'm only staying for two months.'

'*Two months!*' Gegger leans forward to rest a hand on Jamie's shoulder, close enough for him to get a whiff of Gegger's peppery cologne. 'Look, we know we've only just met you, but we have no hesitation in telling you this. You are lovely person. We really like you. Matthew, no.'

'Like I said, he's my friend.'

'*Is* he though?' Pale asks.

On the face of it, Matthew knows far more about Jamie than Jamie knows about Matthew. For all those months, what does he have to show for it? A collection of half-believable stories.

Gegger sits back on the couch, his black velvet undertaker's suit crushed behind guardedly folded arms.

'He's different now,' Jamie concedes.

'You think he was ever interested in you?' Pale asks. 'I can't believe they dragged you out of bed yesterday morning to see the sun come up. You'd been on a plane for thirteen hours, for fucksake.'

'But he's your friend too.'

Gegger snorts. 'Oh brother! Is that what he told you?' He lowers his voice, forcing Jamie even closer. 'We met at an arts festival in Santa Fe. Pale only mentioned we had a shack in the mountains and that was it—couldn't get rid of him. This is only the fourth time we've met him.'

Pale sits forward now, in a persuasive gesture. 'It's so isolated here. Why don't you come back with us, to Sandia Park? At least you'll be closer to Albuquerque.'

'I came all this way to see Taos, to visit my friend. I think I have to give it a chance. After the conversations I've had to-night, I could run screaming into the desert. But I ought not to overreact.'

He remembers what he'd said to Billy. There's no way he's going to go back on his word and have Billy harp on about him being a featherweight. In any case, where the hell would he go? It's the American trip or back to Welston with his tail between his legs. No. Just no.

He tells them about the things Bunni and Steve had said to him. Pale and Gegger stare at him. 'Jamie, we've been talking to that lady,' Pale says, finally. 'The one with the glasses. I think she's in control. She told us about a crazy old machine that she has at her place.'

Gegger takes over, 'This whole story has been documented in *Esoteric Magazine*. They look human. But on their own planet, they manifest as reptiles. Lizards. I think *these* people are *them.*'

Jamie laughs. 'Now you're starting to sound like them.' The feeling of being in danger disappears. 'That machine! How can anyone take it seriously?'

Even Pale has turned to Gegger now with a look of incredulity. 'You don't really believe in all that, do you, Gegger?'

Gegger says, 'Doesn't matter if *I* do or don't. The point is, *they do!* They say they're the oldest living civilized race on Earth. *They* were here before we were.'

Pale shakes his head slowly and pulls an object from his bag, wrapped in tissue. 'For you,' he says.

'From both of us,' Gegger says.

Jamie tears the paper away to reveal a candle in a glass jar. This one has a brightly coloured image of the Virgin Mary emblazoned across one side, not unlike the iconography that adorned the house in London.

'It's the Mary of Guadalupe. We want you to keep this for a time when you need some help,' Pale says.

Jamie frowns. He'd thought they were generally spiritual but not religious. What should he do—risk fate with the lizards or allow himself to be saved by two guys who might also have an agenda?

Gegger shakes his head. 'Not any old trivial problem, like losing your door key or forgetting your mother's birthday.'

Pale takes over. 'No, save this for when something is really getting to you—when you meet with a difficult situation that you just can't get through on your own. Whatever the problem is, write it here,' he taps Mary on the chest. 'Then burn the candle down. Burn it every night until it's gone.

'I know it seems like a strange gift to give to somebody, but if you really won't come with us, we'd like you to have it. Please. Just humour us.' Pale looks over at Matthew in the kitchen. 'At least until you are safely back home.'

Jamie nods. 'Thank you. That means a lot.'

He looks at their sombre faces fixed with horror. 'I'd like us to keep in touch,' he says. 'I'll write and give you a debrief, as soon as I'm home.'

'You'd better,' Pale says.

Would they bother writing back? 'Don't forget to let me have your address before you leave,' he says.

Later, Matthew draws everyone's attention by clinking a spoon on a wine glass. He makes everyone charge their glasses, points in Jamie's direction and makes a toast to him, the new member of their family. Pale and Gegger's glasses remain on the table.

Billy would taunt him over this. This was like one of those daft action-adventure comedies in which one character always ends up unwittingly lost in a desert, or kidnapped by smugglers, in need of rescue by the romantic hero. Well, he doesn't need rescuing. He'll show them all. Later, he'll hold court at dinner parties, quaffing good wine. He'll know about wine, of course. He'll share this moment with his friends. *Academics*. They'll all laugh at the absurdity of it all.

Through the large picture window at the front of the dome, Jamie stares into the blackness of the desert. The red brake lights of Gegger's car burn bright like two hot embers in dwindling fire. If he ran out there now, he wouldn't be too late to stop them. Then Gegger lets the brake off and pulls away so that now only the rear red lamps glow, getting smaller, as they move down the track away from the dome towards the road across the Rio Grande. He is overwhelmed with self-pity, homesickness and terror as they disappear.

§

As Dale drops them in the sleepy town that is Taos, Jamie rubs his temples, his hangover only now beginning to ease. There aren't many people around. Matthew remarks that it's a tourist trap, but to Jamie it appears an out-of-season holiday resort. Shutters cover most of the shop windows and only a few little galleries are open.

'You know, it might be an idea for you to spend more time on your own. You could hitch-hike into town.' Matthew strides ahead. 'You have all this to explore.'

Jamie scampers along the street, a few paces behind. 'What would I do? Everything is boarded up. Why would I come to town on my own? I came here to spend time with you.'

'Don't forget, I do need a bit of time for myself.'

This is cold water in his face but as they reach Cafe Christo, Matthew smiles so widely and in such a friendly manner, Jamie wonders if he'd misheard. 'Deep at my centre is an overflowing pool of love,' he says, repeating one of his affirmations. 'I am safe in the universe. I am at peace wherever I go. I trust life.' He winks and pushes open the door.

A bell above the door jangles. Inside, Shamboo and Prunella are reading the morning newspapers at opposite ends of a long bench with a table each to themselves. Steve serves himself coffee and carrot cake and leaves the cash on the counter. Does this man do any work in a town devoid of crime? Jamie wonders why he's not rushed off his feet with all the UFO landings and alien abductions.

'I'll have a piece of walnut cake and an Earl Grey tea,' Matthew says, taking a seat at Shamboo's table. Jamie seems to be paying for everything. Already he has parted with cash for diesel, alcohol and food for the party. When the waitress returns, Jamie buys drinks and cake, and shyly slips in next to Prunella, who is tapping the seat beside her.

'Lovely to see you again,' she says, shaking the newspaper out in front of her. 'The world is very ill. *Your* time has come.' She pats the paper down and stares into Jamie. 'We waited so long for Matthew. And now *you're* here.'

Steve wipes coffee from his mouth with a serviette. 'Prunella has been channelling the Hermetians for a long time,' he says. 'And then he came.'

Jamie contemplates the validity of her convictions. '*He* doesn't seem to know...'

'He has a little way to go,' Prunella whispers and marks the air in front of her with a pointed finger. 'Like yourself. He's still to let go of a great deal of personal information.' Glancing over at him, it occurs to Jamie that Matthew has already started letting go. He had never called his own mother, not in front of Jamie at any rate, and he never, ever mentioned his family. He'd become remote. Is this what they wanted? Rather than letting go, Jamie had always thought the point of being human was to become more connected, to evolve and share thoughts and ideas until a kind of hive mind could be achieved. Or maybe he'd just been watching too much *Star Trek*.

'Everything alright, dear?' Prunella asks.

Jamie tries to think of a way to ingratiate himself with her. 'You remind me of my grandmother,' he says, finally.

Prunella rubs him gently on the arm and whispers into his ear. 'Did you bring the book?'

Jamie lifts the book from his satchel and sets it on the table. Prunella raises a hand over the worn copy of *The Prophetic Insights*, hovering above the cover. 'You've been busy.'

'I've read it three times,' Jamie says.

'A scholar. But there are more important books to read than just mine. Dip into Betty Shine or Shirley MacLaine.' She opens the book and writes:

> *The divine truth will set you free, Jamie.*
> *Prunella Small*

Jamie thanks her and hides the book away. 'It's odd, don't you think, that you don't really get any 'world' news here?' he says.

'Don't we?' Prunella asks.

'In the UK, we get news reports from all over. Here, the news seems to be very localized.'

'It sounds to me that England is a completely awful place to be at present. There's talk of this "foot 'n' hoof"'

'Foot and *mouth*,' Jamie says. 'It's like flu.'

'And then there's "Mad Cow's Disease". I read only yesterday that there are actually crazy animals walking the streets of England.'

Jamie levels his eyes at this bestselling author. 'The animals are mostly contained in farms. You don't honestly believe—'

She touches him on the hand. 'I like you, Jamie. If there's one thing I respect, it's emotional honesty.' Prunella tilts her head to one side, as if sympathising with a naïve child. Then she looks over at Matthew pontificating.

§

The spite in Matthew's voice has been ringing in Jamie's ears for days. And the days, filled with so much space and so little activity, are long. Jamie sits on Matthew's bed, confronting the mirror wondering how long it would be before they return. It's been five minutes already since they went off in the jeep to run errands. He leans toward his reflection and tugs at an eyelash, pulling it from the space where he has pulled six or seven others, leaving a little gap. He pinches the tiny hair between his thumb and forefinger, and then brings it to his mouth, feeling its end, as sharp as a cactus spine, on his tongue. He resists the urge to pull another and then another until a noticeable break appears in the row of eyelashes. Though as soon as he stops pulling and looks at the vast desert just outside the window, the thoughts rush in again. How did he end up here? What has he got himself into? Why is Matthew behaving so differently? He can't stop the thoughts. Round and round in his head they go. In just a few days, Jamie's heavy-duty reality has become unreliable and nebulous. Every time he allows his mind to dwell upon the situation, his world becomes askew and he feels like running to the toilet.

He presses fingernails into the flesh of his forearm and tries to focus on one real thing at a time. He's in New Mexico, yes. He's here of his own free will, yes. Matthew is his friend and everyone has been nice to him. Yes and yes. They believe in things from another planet. Yes. And Jamie doesn't because those things are lizards. *Lizards.*

Four crescents glow red from where his fingernails dug into the skin—an attempt to keep him in the here and now. He rubs his face, greasy with anxiety. He's twitchy and unable to rest. His mood isn't helped at all by sleep interrupted by a howling animal outside his window. Lizards from another planet. It can't be real.

He lies back on Matthew's bed, staring at the telephone—his only link to world he calls home. If only he'd never started reading those damn books.

He pulls Matthew's duvet up to his neck and clasps the phone to his ear. When he dials Billy's number the first time, there's just the unobtainable tone. He tries again and it rings and rings. Come on, Billy. Please pick up. He leaves it ringing but can't even connect to his answering machine.

After sitting numbly for a minute, he dials his mother's number. He swallows, straightens his back—she's always telling him not to slouch so—takes a breath, ready to deepen his voice—so as not to sound shrill or frantic. Ringing out. Same pattern, no answer, no beep. He *needs* to speak to someone in England, about the mundanity of life, weather, salacious gossip—anything other than crystals, lizards and *Mercury* being in *retrograde*—whatever that means.

Has he brought this upon himself? That's what they'd say.

Every thought we think manifests itself physically. We create our reality.

He makes three more calls—Gracie, David and Auntie Sandra—the only numbers he can remember off the top of his head. He can't get through. It's like being in the Bermuda triangle. He wonders if he might have slipped through a gap in space and time.

Slamming the phone back on its cradle, he stares out of Matthew's window. It frames the emptiness stretching away into infinity. The flat grey of the sky meets the green-grey of the land, reminding him of an abstract painting made on a giant canvas with a roller. Loneliness consumes him. Across the room in the mirror he sees dark circles around his eyes, sunken cheeks; he's wasting away. 'All is well where I am,' he whispers, really needing it to mean something. 'The universe supports me in all that I do. I am surrounded by love.'

'The universe loves you, Jamie.' The voice is unannounced from behind him. Jamie spins round, grasping a pillow to his chest. Matthew stands in the doorway. 'Isn't it beautiful?' he says.

Matthew stares out of the picture window. A fine sprinkling of snow is settling on the ground for as far as it's possible to see.

'Do you think it will get worse?' Jamie asks.

'I guess it could. Imagine, white over. It'll be like a dream—picture postcard.'

§

'Mable Dodge House was once home to artists and writers such as Georgia O'Keefe and D.H. Lawrence,' Matthew trumpeted, tourist guide fashion, when he dropped Jamie off. Now alone, Jamie trudges through the snowy ghost town, towards the most famous adobe building in New Mexico. It's nearest equivalent in England would be a stately home. Leaving Matthew behind for his tarot appointment with Dorothy at Cafe Christo, Jamie tries to focus on something else: his father. Roy had always enthused over the *National Trust Guidebook* when Jamie was a young boy. When he was a teenager they had targeted the castles, houses and ruins of the UK. Mable Dodge House is simply another historic building to add to his list. He remembers vividly the long walks, the hours of staring at exhibits—when, in fact, Jamie had always wanted to go to Butlins. But now the musty smell of the rooms, antiquated books, the linseed of the oil paintings makes him feel closer to Roy. With a close friend or a travelling partner he might enjoy the artwork, the scenery, the atmosphere. Alone, all he can think of is going home. He writes as much as he can in the little journal, knowing that, when this is over, when he finally gets back, he'll want to plunder these emotions, these episodes, for a novel perhaps.

Matthew insisted he would love the house. 'It's full of curiosities that you will find fascinating,' Matthew had said as he pressed a couple of books on to Jamie. Not his thing, at all. He'd once felt an obligation to like the things that Matthew liked but he's given up trying to be so agreeable. He doesn't like the spooky old house.

Alone amongst the relics—an opportunity to reconnect with himself—Jamie searches himself for a fragment, something buried deep within him—an abduction, an arrival, a half-brother. The memory must be there, if it actually *happened*. When Matthew talks about them all 'coming from the stars,' this is what he means. Jamie's seen programmes on television about people who have repressed memories of having been taken in flying saucers, intrusive scientific experiments performed on them. He's waiting for it now, a horrifying flashback of having been violated. He would know if that had happened to *him*. Wouldn't he?

Back outside in the chill air, vapour plumes from his nostrils, as he strides to the Zen Garden, an art gallery supporting Taos painters. The plan was to walk to Taos Plaza where he would meet Matthew and Dale. The anticipation of being with them again makes him feel a little sick. All three of them are to travel to the ancient Indian Pueblo—a museum, as it were, where Native American Indians live as they did before their land was taken. The very idea of it upsets Jamie.

Dragging his feet along the dirt road, Jamie comes across a phone booth. For a moment, less than a moment, his heart springs. Speak to Billy. Though there's the seven-hour time difference. He'll be getting ready for college. Perhaps his mother then? She'll be on her day off. He feels for coins in his pockets, paces up to the booth. Scanning his mind for the international dialling code, a lump forms in his stomach, as he lifts the receiver. A clump of silver now in his fist. It's ringing. A click and a beep and he's emptying coins into the slot.

'Hello.' There it is—his mother's voice.

'Mum!' He pictures Gloria immediately—hand on hip, self-assured, immaculate hair, even for the housework, silk-dressing gown, mules—lounge kitten.

'I was just thinking of you. Couldn't you have called a bit sooner?'

'I tried to call at the beginning of the week. I've had trouble getting through.'

Click-click-click. The phone gulps his money.

'I'm in a phone box.'

'Doesn't Matthew have a phone?'

'I've not got many coins. I just called to let you know I arrived safely.'

'Alright, love,' she says. Her voice is tender and homely. He wishes he could be transported to her right now. 'Save your money. Have a lovely trip.'

'I will.'

'Are you eating properly?'

'Matthew cooked a lovely soup with coriander and ginger.'

'Coriander?'

'They use it in Indian cooking.' Jamie pauses. Breathes deeply. 'Are you okay?'

'Yeah, I'm fine,' she says. 'Why wouldn't I be? Auntie Sandra's coming over for coffee. I think she and Freddie are arguing again. What's the weather like?'

'Oh it's, you know—' He runs out of coins. The line goes

dead. Damn!

Why hadn't he listened to his mother? Why hadn't he gone to Albuquerque with Pale and Gegger?

He sets off for the plaza, assessing the situation. He'll go to the café for some change. He walks across town, snow crunching under his feet, until he sees Matthew outside a bookshop. Jamie walks over to join him. 'Hey. Don't suppose you've got any loose coins?'

Matthew's face contorts into a twist of anger. 'You've not listened to a word I've been saying, have you?' Jamie takes a step backwards. 'I thought I made it clear yesterday. I need time to myself.'

'Matthew—' the word comes out shrill and begging.

Matthew's eyes bulge. 'I can't look after you all the time,' he snarls.

'I don't expect you to,' Jamie says, bracing himself now. 'Matthew, this is ridiculous. I've been reading, writing. Do you really expect me to hitchhike into town? No one around. It's fucking snowing, for Christ's sake. I didn't come all this way because I enjoy travelling. I don't know what strange ideas you and your new friends have got, but this is not a quest. I came to see *you*.'

Matthew might combust. 'I don't think we should talk about this any more.' He turns, walks away from Jamie, down the street.

'Where are you going?'

'Away from you.'

Jamie feels in his pockets for money. He'll be stranded. His passport. All his things are at the dome. 'You can't just leave me here. I don't know what's got into you, but you've changed. You're not—'

'You know who you sound like?' Matthew hisses over his shoulder.

Jamie wants to fly at him. 'You don't know my mother. You don't know the first fucking thing about my mother.'

After travelling back to the dome in silence, Jamie feels hungry. Their meal portions have been so small he feels he needs more food. He doesn't mention it to Matthew. Not now. It crosses his mind that they might be conspiring to weaken him. He goes straight up to the loft, pushes his face into the pillows so they can't hear him sobbing.

Recovering, he sits up on the bed, wiping his eyes, rubbing his damp hands on the bedclothes. Just a half metre away from his fingertips—a dark clump, like a ball of wool. It moves like a brown hairy hand. Then he shoots across the room in sudden terror—a tarantula.

§

From a rock, some two hundred metres away, Jamie can see the dome's interior lights glowing, now that the dusk sun has fallen low on the horizon. The dome seems to pulse and hum ominously, jutting out of the earth like a broken UFO, perhaps surveying his every move, watching him, knowing him. One hundred and eighty degrees of sky, orange to purple, threatens to engulf him. The flat plain of desert, finely textured with loose rocks, stretches out in front of him. The depersonalised feeling of being a speck, a cell in a greater body, fills him with fear. He could disappear from the face of the earth and no one would know.

Jamie shifts uncomfortably inside the warm jacket that Dale lent him for the walk, its papery rustle oddly amplified, in the otherwise deafening silence. He pulls up the collar around his neck, imagining walking in a line from the geodesic dome. His feet and head ache from lack of sleep. As far as the eye can see is a human-less grey-white blanket of snow and frost, interrupted only occasionally by deep faults in the Earth.

There are signs of life dotted about. Matthew told Jamie about the mule deer, the prairie dogs, who roam the scrubland. But he's not in the mood to think of beauty.

He strides back to the dome and shunts open the door. He hangs up Dale's coat and walks around looking for a sign of life, eventually reaching Matthew's bedroom, where the benevolent host welcomes him to join him.

Even though he is free to go wherever he likes—there are no locks, no doors bolted—nowhere is there an available exit route. The dome is a veritable prison.

'I can see it in your eyes.' Matthew smiles kindly, as if the situation at the bookshop hadn't happened. Jamie fully expects him to grow a pair of fangs. They sit on Matthew's bed in front of the large picture window, the way they used to in the house in London on a Sunday morning—Matthew, brewing tea; friendly, warm, safe. 'It frightens you, doesn't it?'

'What?' Jamie says.

'You know, this place can swallow you up if you're not careful. It takes a certain type of person.'

Jamie says. 'Dale told me all the spiders would be hibernating at this time of year. How did it get there?' Jamie's eyes are fixed on the miles of snow-covered desert before them—inches thicker now. A drift has formed against the window. 'I've decided, I can't stay here much longer.' Jamie wraps his fingers around his wrists. 'It's not you. It's me. It's all very exciting, but it's wrong that I'm here. I've come in on the wrong vibration,' he says, throwing in a bit of ingratiating new-age babble.

Even without looking at Matthew, he can feel his incendiary anger. 'You've barely given it a chance.'

'Matthew, I know you think I'm unadventurous, but backpacking, hitch-hiking—it's just not my idea of fun. It's been great to see you. But now I want to go home.'

Matthew's head drops. Jamie turns to face him head on. He needs to look him in the eye for this. When Matthew starts to speak again, his words are slow and deliberate. 'I don't think that's going to be possible now.' He brings his head up and their eyes meet. 'What about the initiation?'

Jamie pauses. 'Matthew—I don't really want to join your thing—whatever it is—I think they're getting me mixed up with someone... something else.'

'How will you get home?'

Jamie shrugs. 'You said that Dale would take me to the airport.'

'Dale has already made arrangements to visit his brother in Colorado,' Matthew says—seeming to enjoy tormenting him.

'If he can take me to Taos, I can get a bus back to Albuquerque. It'll be fine.'

'In this snow? It's far too dangerous.'

'Life doesn't stop in Taos for a layer of snow. Dale drove into town only yesterday.'

'Dale won't be able to take you. You'll have to face the snow, alone.'

'Thirty minutes drive across the desert to Taos?' Jamie says, infuriated. 'Half a day to walk—in the snow—across the Rio Grande. And you said there were bears. I can't walk.'

'Then you'll have to hitch-hike.'

§

The days, like the unending forested sections of skyline, bleed into each other. After trying again, unsuccessfully, to make contact with his mum, Jamie feels beaten. He doesn't have the energy to stand up to Matthew. If Matthew wants to be left alone, then so be it.

Holding his knitting in his fingers, he lifts and presses the soft wool swatch to his mouth and breathes in. Its warm wet llama smell reminds Jamie of home. How he aches now for the safety and familiarity of his grandparents house!

Jamie puts the knitting away, knocks back a cup of brown-green herbal sludge that Matthew brewed for him. He wraps

113

up warm in a thick sweater borrowed from Dale and wrenches on his walking boots. Camera and journal in hand, Jamie cheers goodbye, disguising sullen discomfort, and walks forthrightly up hill towards the woods. Perhaps he'll sit and attempt to write something.

Any life from their nearest neighbour in the trailer home is tucked away inside. Jamie glances over. Other people might be different. He could ask for a lift into town. There's a light on, but no sign of movement. No sound. On other days, he could hear dogs barking. He continues into the brush, towards the aspens, on the crest of the hill.

From up there, the view is something to behold: a desert floor of pastel shades partially covered with frosted shrubs, brittle like pieces of coral.

The dome is just an insignificant dot. He sneers at *them* with their silly stories. How can they know all the answers? When he thinks of the vastness of the universe, the ocean of time that has lapsed since what—say, the big bang, it seems foolish to believe their stories, so inconsequential when you consider the meagre time humans have walked the planet.

A superior race of reptilian overlords governing the universe since long before we were here? To Jamie's mind, any extra-terrestrial race must have evolved at the same time as everything else—from what? Atoms and molecules, algae and other micro-scopic what not. If only he could lie on his mother's sofa now and watch *Coronation Street*.

He kneels and presses his trembling hand against the icy

sand—debris that has been around for thousands of years—pieces of seashell and water-washed stones, marooned miles above sea level. It feels difficult to differentiate between himself and the sand. Flashes of an idea—if everything in the universe is connected, possibly he's made of the same stuff that the sand is made of. The idea comes together in his head like particles of water joining to form a distinguishable vapour. Then he stands and shakes the notion away. In the city, he doesn't feel such things. There he feels like one of the cogs that make everything work. Here, he is nothing—and he is everything, all at the same time.

From the crest he snaps away with his camera, as he's done since he arrived here. There are plenty of pictures of religious buildings, local artists, strange pieces of landscape. He's used rolls of film, recording the whole nightmare. The sound of his camera clicking away is the only thing that can be heard. The remoteness of the place only amplifies his feelings of fear.

Come on, Jamie! He tried to rally himself. He could just get the hell out of here. If he could get to Taos, he could probably get a bus or a coach back to Albuquerque. People do this. Explorers discover continents and climb fucking great mountains in the freezing cold and they survive. Though he struggles to think of a name. *Robert Falcon Scott.* Yeah, but he died, didn't he? Never mind. That's what he will do. He'll pack his things and just fend for himself.

He walks back down the hill, through the sagebrush—startled by the sounds of the dogs now, over at the trailer. He quickens his pace, there being no sign of human supervision. A mix of sand and pebbles slide under his feet. Down the incline, a little too quickly, he stumbles, falls on his knee, sharp pebbles jabbing into his flesh.

The barking grows louder. Dogs don't usually spook him; he's not prone to being harassed by them. One dog is a yappy-snappy little creature: the other looks like a wolf. He brushes himself off, breathes deeply and walks on, deliberately steady this time, so as not to entice them into a game of chase. They continue to bark, less than a hundred yards from him. He's mindful not to make eye-contact. Louder. He turns. Closer. The wolf is upon him, growling and baring its teeth—blue eyes, piercing. It pads the ground, and then leaps forward.

'Stop!' Jamie shouts. Then more softly, 'I'm not going to hurt you.' He bows his head trying to appear docile, hoping the owner will come and round them up. No one appears. The wolf dog runs at him, snarling and foaming at the mouth.

A spark of fear—suddenly he's detached from his body, hovering above himself, watching the dog. He pushes it off, swings his camera on the end of its leather strap. It misses the dog.

He runs for the dome, too far away, slipping on pebbles, jumping over rocks—the dog just behind. Faster. Teeth sink into his leg. He screams, cries out for help. It bites—bites again, drawing blood, tearing his trousers. Pain. A jolt. A stone in his hand. Misses. Stumbles backwards, arms flailing frantically

The dog snarls—leaping—fangs just missing his face. Jamie pushes it away, fingers inside its mouth. 'Fuck off, fuck off!' Its teeth, needles through flesh. Saliva loose from its tongue hits Jamie's cheeks. He falls. Hits his head on hard rock. Hands search blindly for another stone. Seizing a jagged piece of rock, he stabs at the dog's side, inducing a painful yelp. It backs away.

A strange filmic sensation of being an observer, while at the same time, being observed—makes Jamie feel a presence other than the dog. Is he hallucinating? A twinge of remorse condenses in his mind before the dog snarls again.

On his feet now, exhaustion overcomes Jamie. The dog licks the bloody wound in its side. Jamie takes this chance. He gallops toward the dome. At the threshold, he glances back; the dog has vanished. He collapses emotionally, just for a moment and feels himself jerk, like a television regaining its signal, back into his body. Seeing through his own eyes, in his own skin, he sobs. The wounds beneath his trouser leg—blood, teeth-marks. He touches his head—battered.

He staggers into the wooden antechamber, locking doors behind him. The inner door into the living area is open. He looks into the kitchen, expecting to find Matthew cooking. Silence.

Slowly regaining perspective, he breathes, wanting to leave the drama outside. Maybe Matthew is napping. Jamie kicks off his wet shoes and suppresses his urge to cry.

In the living room, he pulls off clothes. He spots eight red flashing lights dotted around on the carpeted area of the dome and becomes slowly aware of a very low-pitched vibrating hum. The lights were not there before; not when he left. Just get out of these bloody clothes. He pulls Dale's sweater over his head and, steps further into the room. There they are, Dale, Matthew, Prunella and Bunni, on opposite sides of the dome, cross-legged in what looks like a deep meditative trance—all of them, eyes closed.

Close to blacking out now, his thundering heartbeat slows dramatically. His vision greys. He gently moves the door towards its frame but at the last second decides to let it slam, making his presence known. They don't move. What the fuck are they doing—invoking spirits? They don't even appear to be breathing. The vibrating continues.

'Matthew?' he calls across the room. Even his freaky fucking eyelids are still. Jamie stares at his face; it appears to shift for a second. His features undulate—not bones or the muscles, it's the flesh of his face itself, moving independently of the structure beneath. Now more. Cheekbones swell; the chin becomes subtly elongated. The shiny flesh on his forehead ripples, the beginnings of horns pushing through angry red skin like hot boils. Jamie wants to scream but no sound emerges. He's still dizzy—drunk, even.

Matthew opens his eyes. Behind the lids, his eyes have rolled back so that only the whites show. They roll forward again and flicker from side to side.

Jamie is transfixed. He wants to look away but his eyes are hooked on Matthew's lips which part into a thin opening, through which slides a repulsive green tongue, long and forked. What the fuck is that vibrating hum? He feels a stomach cramp and wretches on the floor in front of him. Then—blackness.

No humming. When Jamie opens his eyes, his vision is filled by the image of Prunella Small kneeling over him—a mass of white curls. Her large blue glasses hang precariously on the end of her nose.

'Matthew said you'd popped out for a stroll. What happened?' she asks. 'You've been gone for hours.'

It takes a few moments before Jamie can orientate himself. Is he imagining this? 'I got bitten by a dog.'

Matthew sneers, towering over both of them. Lying on the floor of the dome, Jamie tugs up his trouser leg, showing them his wounds. Prunella rises, stands back and folds her arms.

'You've brought it all upon yourself,' Matthew says.

'Matthew!' Jamie says, pushing himself up, onto his elbows.

Prunella purses her lips. 'If it's sympathy you want, you've come to the wrong place.'

'Aren't you going to do something? I need some antiseptic.'

Prunella, Dale, Matthew and Bunni move in on him. Collectively, speaking in unison—'Every thought we think makes our universe.'

Their eyes roll back into their heads and they chant, reciting words and sounds that Jamie cannot decipher.

§

'Yes, I'm well aware that the departure date is over a month away, but now I need an earlier flight.' Jamie's stomach churns. 'Aren't there any flights to London at all this week?' Inside his mind:

119

a black abyss. A sensation that often creeps up on him without him realising. It's the same sensation that overcame him at school, where he was relentlessly bullied. It was the dull leaden helplessness that came when he realised his mother might die of meningitis or when his parents were fighting, and he had to go and live with his grandparents, Phyllis and Alf, for a week. It will pass. It usually passes, with sleep, with the conversation of a close friend. But this is heavier than usual. Tears fill his eyes and his throat, and he struggles to suppress the *what if*.

'I'm sorry, sir,' the voice of the reservations assistant says. 'Could you read the ticket number to me again?'

Jamie does so, twice more. He clutches the blankets on the edge of Matthew's bed.

'Sir, I'm sorry but there's no record of this number logged in our system. It might be a printing error. If you paid with a credit card, I should be able to trace the booking.'

'I have it here.' Jamie runs a finger across the embossed plastic numbers, reminding himself that he's here, now. He reads each one carefully, holding his breath between each number.

The enormity of the silence at the end of the phone line is held back by a tiny glimpse of light. He waits on the brink of good news; his stomach uncoils slightly.

'I'm really sorry, sir. I can't help you. There's no trace of your ticket number *or* your credit card booking on the computer system.'

Jamie's mind bungees back into the abyss. 'I have it here in my hand. Flight AB132 to Houston, flight LG495 to Gatwick.'

'I'd really like to help you, but there is no flight AB132. It doesn't exist.'

He's going to throw up. Just breathe. He rubs the sharp edge of the plastic card against the soft flesh on the inside of his forearm, leaving angry pink tramlines. When he returns home, he'll start a steady job, spend the rest of his life holidaying in the Med, eat boring food and numb out on crap television just like ordinary people do.

'I can sell you a new ticket, sir. I can make a booking for you now over the telephone.'

'You don't understand.' Jamie's voice cracks. He looks at the bedroom door, hoping he won't be interrupted. 'I don't have any more money. I assumed everything would be... I bought the tickets all together. I still have the boarding pass for my outbound journey.'

'Mister Johnson, I can only suggest that you bring the ticket, along with your credit card to the airport. Perhaps it *is* a printing error.'

'Can you guarantee that I'll get a seat on the plane?'

'Let me check availability for when you might be travelling.' Jamie listens to the sound of fingers running across plastic computer keys. 'Mister Johnson, all flights on Friday, Saturday and two flights on Sunday are fully booked.'

'And in the next three weeks?'

'There are often cancellations. I'm sorry I can't be more helpful.'

When he puts down the phone, Jamie wants to curl up and

weep. His mind falls, this time without a safety line, back into that black hole. He sees one image in his mind far, far away. Almost an indistinct dot: his mother.

§

Gloria isn't home, so Jamie takes advantage of the line in Matthew's bedroom actually working to make another call.

'Jamie! You need to calm down,' Billy says.

'I'm terrified of finding more spiders!' Jamie nervously scans the bed sheets for arachnids, thinking better of mentioning what happened the other afternoon. He's still not sure if he has been dreaming, drugged, or else experiencing something quite out-of-this-world. All he can think of is getting away from these freaks.

'You were right, Billy,' he speaks quietly into the receiver. 'I should have listened to you. I should have listened to Mum.'

'Well, don't think about that now.' The line is so clear, Billy could be in the next room. 'You've enough to think about without beating yourself up.'

The dog bites are healing, slowly. He hooks his fingernail underneath the edge of a scab, until fresh blood seeps out and he feels a twinge of pain. This helps to focus his mind.

'Don't waste your holiday time. Go to New York, Jamie. Just get on a plane.'

Jamie hears footsteps. 'I'd better go, Billy. Someone's coming.'

'Wait.'

'It's not a good time.' Jamie can sense Matthew on the other side of the door.

Billy's voice gets louder. 'What's going on?'

'I'll call you soon,' Jamie says.

'Jamie. Wait!'

'What?'

'I love you—'

'I love you too, Billy.' The line is dead. 'Billy?'

§

Jamie waits for them to go out for their afternoon walk. Then he follows the telephone cable along the skirting-board into the darkened spare room. He's keen and alert. He breathes steadily. Pressure builds on him, while on his knees, tracing the cable. They won't be gone long. Why is this phone line so unpredictable? One minute it's working, the next it's dead.

It's hard to see in this dimness. Jamie stands and switches on the light. He sees a second telephone on a little table. He walks over and picks it up—listens. There's that perfectly clear *brrrrrrrr* ringtone. A different line? He places the receiver down and kneels. Next to the table is the end of the line to the phone he's been trying to use, the end of it completely free of the socket.

§

Initiation? Healing machines? There's no way they're getting him to go to that woman's house. If he's quick, he can be out of here before they come back. He doesn't know if he should pack the big rucksack or not. He doesn't want another confrontation with Matthew. No. The big rucksack will draw too much attention. He kicks it under his bed and packs his small holdall instead—just the essentials: reading material, waterproofs, camera, passport, plane tickets, money, the candle given to him by Pale and Gegger and his notebooks. There's nothing amongst the remaining things that he can't obtain again in London. He'll leave in the clothes he's standing up in and slip away unnoticed into the night. Are there really bears out there, or have they told him this in order to keep him prisoner?

Jamie arranges things in the holdall, hands shaking from a mixture of nerves and low blood sugar. Has he got everything? He looks round the room at his stuff scattered untidily around the room. Check. Check. No, he's forgotten something. He remembers his camera. Must take that. He finds it lying on a chest of drawers. Just as he's placing it carefully into the bag, he hears Matthew's voice. 'I've been meaning to have a word with you about that.' Jamie looks up and catches Matthew staring at him from the doorway. 'The camera. I expect Prunella would love some good pictures of the event.'

Jamie is speechless. Now what? He'll have to go with them.

'Are you ready?' Matthew asks.

Jamie looks out of the window at the desert. The dirt road leading to Taos still visible even under light snow. In trembling hands, Jamie turns, lifts his camera to his eye and shoots Matthew.

§

In her basement, Prunella sits, large thick-lensed glasses balancing on the bridge of her nose, needles rhythmically clicking like the sound of woodland insects.

'Ah, you came,' she says, as Jamie steps down into the sparse room. 'No Matthew?'

Jamie doesn't want to talk about the tension between himself and Matthew. What good would it do? 'I left him upstairs. I came to see you alone. You're knitting?'

Prunella holds up the mass of webby green wool. 'A shawl.'

'My grandmother taught me when I was a little boy.'

'And I taught my grandson,' she says, a sad lilt of remorse in her voice. 'I don't see him now, I…'

'She used to pick up my stitches when they unravelled.' He feels tears in his eyes. He wants to see her so much.

'I've had to let go. We *all* have to let go. But… you remind me of him.'

She puts down her knitting and turns his attention to her treasured possession. 'I thought you ought to see this.'

In the middle of a white room fitted with chrome units sits the *machine*—a computer—all screens, knobs and buttons, inside a curtain of translucent surgical-green plastic. Next to the machine is something like a dentist's chair upholstered in white

PVC. It's surrounded by breathing apparatus, electrodes and a monitor screen.

'Isn't it wonderful? Your reading will be displayed here and we'll be able to see where all the imperfections are.'

The sight of it all chills Jamie's blood. Is this what they have in store for him? They're going to strap him on that thing. He imagines himself wrestling with them—Matthew, Dale, the others, holding him down.

Jamie forces a smile. He's knows he's leaking emotions from every corner of his face. He can't fool Prunella. 'And then what?' he asks.

'We will make you complete,' Prunella says. 'The way you were before you were incorporated on Earth without the flaws you have now.'

Jamie scans the room for another exit. It's a cellar: there is only the doorway he's standing in.

'It's perfectly safe, Jamie. Imagine, we're just returning you to your factory settings. You'll feel a little dizzy at first. The whole experience will accelerate the spinning of your own chakras.' Prunella strokes her hands across the shiny white surface of the chair. 'We've all been done. But you, Jamie, you will benefit the most.'

Jamie edges into the room to get a better look. He wonders what it would feel like to erase it all: the bullying at school, all his neuroses, all the shit that haunts him. What a relief it might be to let go of all that weight. But this is all hocus-pocus, isn't it?

'You'll have to be naked of course. You have a problem with

that?' Her head is cocked slightly to one side, a contradictory earnest look in her opal eyes.

Jamie feels his face fixed like marble. Prunella softens. 'It's not easy, honey. We all feel we need that personal connection,' she says.

Prunella looks down at the web of knitting in her lap. While she'd been talking to him, her stitches had all fallen off the needles. 'Oh darn it,' she says. 'Stupid. Stupid. My eyesight is not what it should be. I'll never get all this back on the needles.'

Jamie bends over her to investigate. The tangle of loose wool presents a challenge for him—something he can do for her. 'Let me try,' he says.

'Oh, I'm not sure you'll be able to—'

He lifts the knitting swiftly out of her hands and in seconds he's settled on the floor next to her, carefully picking up each stitch, one by one and returning them to the needles. He spreads the stitches along the needle and checks to see if he's missed anything and then carefully hands it back to her.

'You treasure,' Prunella says. She looks at him as if she's saying goodbye for a very long time. It feels right, for some strange reason. Prunella leans forward and kisses him on the cheek. It feels like a kiss that has waited a long time to be planted.

'I think I better get back upstairs to help Matthew,' Jamie says.

§

Dale, Bunni and everyone else are in the kitchen, preparing for the party, assembling paper lanterns and unpacking glasses. On the surface of one of the preparation areas sits a bottle of brown-green herbal sludge, labelled *Yagé*. It has the same devious appearance of the tea Matthew had made him drink before being bitten by that damned dog. Through the window, Jamie can see Matthew is outside moving fence posts to make space for the extra guest vehicles that will arrive tomorrow evening. The road where Prunella's house stands has been gritted and cleared of snow.

A moment of clarity, blade-sharp, hits Jamie. Absolutely no good can come from any of this: the violation, the manipulation, his own puerile behaviour. He needs to be back home with Billy. It's the most awake, the most grown-up he's felt since he arrived here. He'll confront Matthew and tell him that they must take him to the bus station. They can't keep him here, a prisoner. He darts through Prunella's kitchen, and outside. As Jamie approaches, Matthew is trying to move a boulder from the gravel driveways.

Matthew turns his back, pulls up the collar on his jacket. Even in this weather, he's still wearing those daft shorts, exposing his yellow knees to the elements. 'I have nothing to say to you, Jamie.'

Jamie is expecting this. 'Well, *I* have something to say to *you*.'

Matthew is scraping earth from underneath the boulder with a kitchen knife, trying for more leverage. Don't they have a shovel? A trowel? As Jamie steps towards him, Matthew spins—the knife in his outstretched hand, whistling through the air. 'Get away from me,' he screams.

'Why are you so angry?' Jamie dodges.

Matthew's eyes are on fire. 'You've done nothing but *take* from us.'

'That's rich! *Me* taking from *you?*'

'From the moment you got off the plane you wanted to stir up trouble between Dale and myself.'

'Where the hell has this come from?' Jamie gasps. 'You're delusional.'

Matthew continues his blind rant, conjuring up stories about what he thinks has been going on during Jamie's stay. By some vindictive sleight of hand, the impression he was giving was that instead of being invited here, Jamie had somehow wheedled his way in and had been trying to take advantage. 'And that energy you ooze,' Matthew hissed. 'It's so damaging.'

'Oh, you know,' Jamie begins quite frankly, 'the energy thing—it's gone far enough now.'

'Your negativity is putting the entire project at risk,' Matthew says.

'I had no idea I had such power.' Jamie laughs. It's the first time he's really laughed in weeks. 'You've brought me here under false pretences.'

The knife is just inches away from his face. '*You* wanted this,' Matthew says. 'I opened a door for you.'

'Yeah, you *opened* a door. I was in awe of you. You made me think it was *your* life that I wanted, sitting around in cafes all day long with a notebook. I thought you were going to teach me how to beat the system, not give me bullshit about extra-terrestrials before strapping me to a machine to have my DNA poked and prodded.'

'Ungrateful wretch!'

Jamie eyes him defiantly. 'Certainly pulled the wool over my eyes, didn't you? Making me think you knew all those people—David, Gracie and the rest of them.'

The knife moves even closer; Jamie doesn't flinch. 'I should never have chosen you,' Matthew hisses. *Chosen him?* Again, he sees an image of himself strapped into that hideous machine, flashing through his mind.

'I'm your friend. Stop being ridiculous. How you got yourself mixed up in this nonsense, I'll never know.'

Matthew lunges, the point of the knife quivering just a hair's breadth away from Jamie's face, causing him to lose his footing and fall.

Scrambling around on the muddy driveway, Jamie feels his arse cut by grit and salt. Looming over him, Matthew's face bends. Reality distorts like a funfair mirror. The knife becomes liquid. Matthew's eyes become sacks of blood. His face reddens, temples swelling and undulating just where horns might grow. Jamie's seen this before. He closes his eyes for just a moment, hoping that this is all a—

It's not going to go away. When he opens his eyes, the bones protrude where Matthew's temples are, the skin—leathery and shiny with beads of sweat.

He refuses to let his own mind turn on him. But his vision buckles. He might vomit. A lizard in the shape of a man—forked tongue, flickering eyes—lurches forwards, now thrusting the knife right at Jamie. Misses. Jamie screams, voice cracking, leaving just air hissing over vocal chords. Jamie scrambles to his feet. Pushes Matthew away. They tussle. Buttons tear from Matthew's coat. Runs back to the house. Where else to run?

'He's trying to kill me,' he shrieks, running right into the kitchen-diner, scattering place settings, glasses, vases of flowers.

Prunella spins round with her knitting in her hand. The green ball of wool falls and rolls across the floor. 'What in the name of—'

'You're all fucking crazy,' Jamie screams, knocking crockery out of Dale's hands. Plates and glasses clatter to the floor.

'What's wrong, dear?' Prunella stands there in her tracksuit bottoms, arms wide now, the knitting dangling. She looks at Dale as he reaches for broken plates on the floor. 'He was fine a few minutes ago. I don't know what's got into him.'

Jamie points at them all. 'I know what you're doing.' He gags, barely able to breathe, heart pounding. 'I should have listened to them.'

'Calm down!' Prunella calmly takes off her blue rimmed glasses and rubs them on her cardigan. 'Dale, get him a chair,' she says, replacing her glasses on the bridge of her nose.

Jamie recoils. 'Don't any of you come near me!'

'He's in shock.' Prunella says to Dale.

'I just want to go home!'

'Hush a minute,' Prunella says. 'I can't think with all your hollering.'

'I need to get out of here.' Jamie cries.

'You can't just leave us now,' Dale says. 'Don't you want to be welcomed into our family?'

'I have my own fucking family!' How can he connect with them? Nothing he says will make them hear him. 'I want to see mother, I want to see my grandmother, please…'

'No one is holding you prisoner,' Prunella says.

'But you are!' Jamie laughs hysterically. 'It's fucking snowing. They refused to take me to the bus stop.' He points at Dale. 'I can't *walk* across the desert.'

Matthew walks in now, face congenial, no sign of the knife.

'Is this true, Matthew?' Prunella says. 'Did he ask for your help?'

Matthew shrugs. 'You want us to let him go, before tomorrow's initiation?'

Prunella presses a hand to her head. 'This is a reality *you* have created, Jamie. This is what you must have wanted for yourself.'

It dawns on him. He *had* made this real. It was a sick fantasy nurtured by loneliness that began long ago. But from that fantasy he'd plagiarised more sick fantasies. Whatever he'd thought was going on is not what was going on at all. He wants to go back and rewrite the script. A multitude of thoughts race through his mind. What the hell has he been doing? He should be at home now, working on a novel, looking for an agent—not wasting his time in the desert.

'I even called the airline but they have no record of my booking!'

'You're being selfish,' Prunella says. 'After all our hard work? The least you could do is stay for the party.'

Jamie shakes his head. She hasn't seen what he had seen. Was she aware of Matthew's behaviour? 'I want to go home.' He can feel himself unravelling—yarn free of needles. But now there's no-one to pick up the stitches for him.

Prunella looks down at the length of knitting in her hands. Then up to Jamie again. 'That's settled.' She stoops for the ball of wool and starts to wind it back up. 'Tomorrow morning. Dale will drive you to the bus stop.' She looks at Dale, 'No buts,' and then at Jamie, 'What company are you flying with?'

'Continental.'

Prunella looks out of the kitchen window, as if consulting some higher source. Outside it's beginning to snow again. 'Okay... okay...' She looks back at Jamie. 'There'll be a seat on the Continental. An afternoon flight. I'd say around five o'clock. You'll need to rise early if you're to get a bus from outside the Taos Inn.'

Matthew scowls. 'We can't just let him...'

'He's of no use to us now,' Prunella says.

'We must press ahead with the initiation.'

Prunella laughs. He is trying to take the upper hand. 'Even more zealous than usual, Matthew.' She turns on him. 'I said, he's of no use to us now. If there's one thing I can't cope with, it's negativity.' She glances at Jamie and smiles.

He feels his world coming to an end. Who can he trust now? Matthew makes a grab for Jamie, and Jamie sees it again—the tip of that forked tongue. With a brief flash of bravery, he dashes out into the blizzard.

§

A spectator in his own movie, Jamie is running as fast as his feet will carry him. He's lost track of time. Hard salt-like snow bites into his face. White biscuit crunches beneath his feet. He snatches a look behind him. Alone, thank *fuck*—he must be miles from the house by now. Before him the road leads through a thick wooded area and beyond, what he assumes is the Rio Grande. The sun is sinking behind the trees. The day is closing in. His breath freezes into white spirits.

The dangers—the bears, the drop in temperature, the distance he might have to cover to reach the bus garage—running away was perhaps not the most sensible choice. But what choice does he have?

It might take him all night to find his way in the dark. Could they follow his tracks? This thought forces him off the road and he dives into the woods, where the floor has been protected from the snow by the brush and the aspen. His trail is no longer visible as he rushes on through the damp mulch. Only a trained hunting dog could come after him now.

The setting sun casts the vertical prison bars of the aspen into silhouette. He's determined to reach the other side before the light fades. Cold air burns the back of his throat. On the other side of the woods, he perceives the beam of headlights along the distant carriageway. What will he do at the road? He has none of his things with him. Why did he ever come here in the first place? Why didn't he listen to his mother?

Closer to the road, the air is filled with a revolting stench. Catching his foot on a log, he tumbles headfirst into snow, inches away from the dead thing. He is jolted into the present.

Now has never been so vivid. The world clarifies: a mangle of disfigured fur, snout, teeth, bloody broken ribs, crushed, flattened limbs, lies decomposing. A bear, road-kill crushed by the wide tyres of a truck, rotting at the edge of the carriageway.

Car headlights throw a beam onto the carcass, followed by the screech of tyres. The passenger door is flung open. Prunella looks over the rims of her glasses from the driving seat. 'You want to get eaten by one of those things?'

'I'm not going back there,' Jamie shouts. 'You can't make me.' He runs in the opposite direction, into the driving snow. Behind him, he hears the revving engine, and the vehicle slammed into gear. She drives alongside him again, the open door almost swinging off its hinges.

'Are you out of your fucking mind? You'll die in this weather. Get in.'

Jamie holds his hands up. 'I'm going home.'

'Time to put the stitches back on your needles,' she says.

'What?' Jamie feels an almost hypodermic rush of relief.

'Trust the universe, sweetie.' She indicates something in the back seat—the bag he'd left at her house. Then picks up something from the passenger seat and holds it up.

'My passport!'

'Jamie, when you're so close up to an idea, most of the time you can't see its true significance. Is it new? Is it old? Only when you get some distance from it do you fully comprehend it.'

Jamie shivers.

'I'm packing you off.'

'What about Matthew?'

'He and I will be having words.'

§

Across a brown-white canvas of desert, Jamie rides a small bus equipped with snow-chains. It climbs up steep roads through the night and once again into bright blue skies. He's lost a friend, a bad one. But it still feels as if he's leaving something behind. He remembers remains of the bear—drags a sharpened thumbnail down the inside length of his forearm, bringing up a welt of pink flesh, angry enough to trap him in the present.

Just as Prunella had predicted, there *is* a seat for him on the Continental. A last minute cancellation frees up a single window seat, as if the universe had rearranged itself for his journey home. And they exchange his ticket with no hiccups.

The lady in the seat next to him tries to make polite conversation several times. Eventually, he pretends to be asleep. He needs to decompress. But images flash behind his eyelids—the desert, the snow, Matthew. His voice says, 'We're all from the stars.' Jamie opens his eyes. Through the window he can see a velvety blue blanket pricked with glittery dots whose essence may, in fact, be contained within him, but whose light is long gone.

§

Gloria's nearly done the housework—the vacuuming, the washing. She's only to put away the laundry, walk the dogs and do a spot of dusting, then she's done. Everything is in its place. She arranges two candlesticks on the fireplace with an eye on symmetry. She uses a feather duster and a hairdryer on her silk flower arrangement.

On top of the TV is a china Pierrot clown sculpture that Jamie bought her when he was little. Bless. Saved up all his pocket money. Lifting it gently in one hand, she dusts it and places it back. Just a centimetre to the left. She's been like this all her life—taking care of everything. She's had that clown for years and there's not a mark on it. She doesn't like anything to get ruined.

It reminds her of the time when she had to go to the eye infirmary, as a child, to have a squint corrected. The pain was excruciating and she cried for days. Phyllis bought her a set of china dolls to cheer her up. They had beautiful satin dresses, realistic hair and carefully painted faces. She kept them on a shelf in her room. Sometimes, she would sleep with one. One day she came home from school to find them all lined up on her bed, spectacles drawn on them with a ballpoint pen. Her favourite, the one with the red hair had a moustache and a pince-nez. Bleeding Sandra. She always lost interest in her own little trollops and had to deface Gloria's.

The sound of a parcel through the letterbox, falling with a heavy thwack, brings her back. It brings a smile to her face. She tears open the brown paper packaging to reveal the catalogue from the cruise ship holiday company that she'd ordered a couple of weeks ago. Time she and Roy broke out of the mould.

§

The fatty sludge of the in-flight meal reminds Jamie of the road-kill he'd seen. Its pieces will be carried away by the beetles, washed into the ground by the rain, perished by frost, blown away by the wind until nothing remains. But it must still exist. Each microscopic piece of it, every molecule, every atom, redistributed to the universe. He can imagine himself, disintegrating like the bear, returning to the nebula. We're all particles of carbon, hydrogen, whatever, and everything in the universe is made of the same stuff. We are all one and the same thing. He feels his mind expand like elastic, suddenly reassured by the permanence of life.

§

'I'm not having it, Roy,' Gloria says, three steps ahead of the shopping trolley. The sun, low in the sky, casts a long shadow on the car park. 'It's gone downhill ever since that new manager started.' Gloria glances over her shoulder at Roy, who is angling the trolley to compensate for the camber of the tarmac. Such an expert. 'Two luncheon vouchers for the Wacky Warehouse—do they really think that's recompense for what they've put me through?'

Roy sighs, as they reach the car. 'You've got your money back, haven't you?'

'It's the inconvenience, Roy. And I won't be made a fool of. Did you see the look that cashier gave me? Smug bitch.'

Roy opens the rear door so they can chuck the carrier bags in the back. 'Don't upset yourself, love. Come on, we'll pick up fish and chips on the way home.'

'You have fish if you want,' she says. 'I think I'll have one of them shish-kebabs. I feel like something exotic.' She's organizing the shopping in the back of the car, moving items from one bag to another. 'Roy, what have I told you about putting the washing machine powder next to the salad? You'll have us all poisoned.'

Roy holds up something that she's snuck into one of the salad bags.

'Oh, that. It's just coriander,' she says, as if it were something dull and everyday like a jar of Branston Pickle.

'Is it foreign?'

Why does he do this—raw meat next to a bottle of Domestos?

'You could say that. They use it in Indian and Thai cooking. Thought I'd give it a whirl.'

They drive in silence for a mile or so until Roy reaches the industrial estate near to where they usually pick up supper. The road runs adjacent to an old factory covered in graffiti and barbed wire. The *Glasshouse Gentleman's Health Spa* is set in what looks like an old public house. Gloria waves her hand irritably, indicating that Roy should slow down.

'If I go any slower I'll get done for kerb crawling.'

'Don't be ridiculous,' she says. 'Not with me in the passenger seat. Just stop, outside the gates. I want to get a better look.'

'A better look?'

'I'm just curious. Nothing wrong with that, is there?'

Roy pulls up in front of the building.

'I tell you something, Roy. They must be making a mint here. Pink Pound they call it. Look at the cars on that car park.'

'I'm surprised there's much call for it round here, Glo.'

'Sandra says it's all married men what use it. Swingers.'

'I'll bet it's awash with disease,' Roy laughs.

'You keep away. D'you hear?' She giggles. 'I can do without crabs at my age.'

Roy tuts. 'As if.' He revs the engine.

She prods his legs with a fingernail. 'And don't mention it to our Jamie when he's back here. I don't want him getting ideas.'

Roy pulls away. 'Don't knock it, Gloria. After everything, he might be safer there than anywhere else.'

§

Jamie is disturbed by the muffled noises of Camden Town floating through the front door of Billy's bedsit, up the stairwell and under the duvet. He hears the door slam. Billy's footsteps. It feels like he's been asleep for days. The homely smell of Billy's cigarette brings him to a halfway state between sleep and wakefulness. Next thing he knows, Billy is above him with kisses and a mug of hot chocolate. 'How are you feeling?'

'I think I should go and stay with Mum and Dad.' Jamie feels maimed.

'Commute to the gallery? Don't be ridiculous. Why don't we get a little place together?'

Jamie sits up in bed. 'Buy? That's a big jump from sofa-surfing in student digs.'

'I've been looking at a few places. Dalston. It would be cheaper than renting and it would be ours. Our own little piece of London. I can't see you lasting long at your mother's.' Billy leans over and kisses him. 'There's a letter. Postmark *New Mexico*.' He sits down on the bed.

Jamie tears open the envelope. 'It's from Pale. I gave him *your* address. Don't want any mail going to my mother, eh?'

Dearest Jamie,

For sure you must be home by now. I know you won't be able to stand those creeps for long. I only hope your heart is in one piece. You're in the small percentage of people who see and feel with their hearts. Just keep hold of the thought—everything happens for a reason. Back home, you'll start making sense of everything. Matthew must have had something very unhappy and cruel happen to him to have got himself involved in this nonsense. A lot of times, people do not survive their past and are unable to heal. We are not lizards! Our tails do not grow back when they fall off. When it all gets too much for me, I go out in town to breathe and dance with the neighbourhood dogs.

I have to say, I was not very thrilled to meet you at first. I thought only a creep must hang out with them, but I was incredibly wrong. You are not at all a miserable or negative person. But clearly you had no idea what you were being led into. I was never comfortable around either of them. Matthew has monsters living in his head and Dale is just a bore.

You know, we had no idea that they wanted to stay the night. How absurd, to turn up like that and take over our kitchen! Rest assured, Gegger and I had it all worked out. We were both sure they were in a cult. And the good thing is, you and I have a friendship created out of darkness. Highly dramatic things seem to happen to people like us. And dragons are attracted to angels.

Write, as soon as you get home and tell me everything.

Love Pale x

§

Jamie looks at the bank clerk in disbelief.

'What do you mean, 'Could *I* have authorized these

transactions?' The money had been taken out of his account yesterday, in *dollars*. 'I've been back a week.' He can't afford to be further overdrawn.

'Can you verify the following transactions for me...' The clerk turns the monitor screen to Jamie: *Human Light Research. BioGasVisCorp. GDVsystemtech.co.* The dates of the transactions and the names of the businesses don't tally with any places he'd actually visited. His mind races. The card was never out of his sight. He knows that much. He thinks of the spider in his bed, the disconnected telephone. He wouldn't put anything past them.

'Have you reported your card lost or stolen?'

'I didn't authorize these transactions. I need you to put that money back in my account.'

'We can only assume that the card was cloned while you were in America.'

'Cloned?'

'Criminals sometimes use devices that copy the information off the magnetic strip. This enables them to make an exact replica of your card.'

'But how would they know my pin number?'

'They don't need it to buy stuff from the internet. I need to speak to the manager about this. We'll keep the account active in order to investigate the problem.'

§

Billy is lying on the bed channel hopping. Something catches Jamie's eye. The scenery, then whiteness, a plastic curtain—the camera pans, a dentist's chair. Billy hops again.

'Put that back.' Jamie jabs a finger at the television screen.

'It's just some crap documentary.'

Jamie wrenches the remote from Billy's hands. 'Listen.'

The narrator describes a cult in New Mexico who believe themselves to be the children of a group of enlightened beings, from a star system on the other side of the universe. 'This is it, Billy. That's the place,' Jamie says, shaking Billy's leg.

The documentary reports members recruiting in the UK, convincing young people to initiate themselves in the desert near Taos, New Mexico. They believe originally they had an extra strand of DNA, which got lost when the *children* manifested on earth. A special machine perfects their humanized bodies. And the thing that strikes home to Jamie—the narrator reports the building of vast funds, conning new recruits out of thousands of pounds. The gay communities of London, Berlin, New York and San Francisco have become targets of the cult because it's believed that people of a homosexual orientation have less 'personal information' to hamper their induction: fewer family bonds and paternal links mean a smoother initiation to the *family*.

Jamie's mind shoots back to the morning he met Matthew for the first time. 'How could I have been such a fool?' he says. Now on the television a distorted home video sequence, intermittently interrupted by static. Roaming footage reveals the machine room Jamie had stood inside. Jamie and Billy watch a naked woman strapped into the dentist chair, electrodes all over her body. Figures in white protective suits spectate. She's writhing around in pain.

'This is going to give me fucking nightmares,' Billy says, grabbing the remote control. 'Turn it off.'

'No.'

The narrator explains that the group use dangerous sleep-inducing delta waves to slow the heartbeat of the victims they wish to incapacitate. Then they can reveal themselves in their purest form. These lizards feed off negative energy produced by humans.

'Makes sense. They made out that they couldn't stand my pessimism but they deliberately pushed me into a situation in which I was terrified.'

'You don't really believe this shit, do you?' Billy says.

'Have you got a lighter?' Jamie is out of bed and rummaging in a drawer.

'You haven't started smoking?' Billy asks.

Jamie finds the candle tucked inside a pair of Superman underpants.

'What?'

'The Mary of Guadeloupe.'

§

'Jamie. They're here,' Gloria calls up the stairwell. She primps before the hallway mirror and then opens the front door. The puffiness under her eyes betrays disturbed sleep last night. 'Alright Sandra?'

'Alright Glo?' Sandra is wearing a strappy red, white and blue sequined top the pattern of a Union Jack. Taking fashion advice from Ginger Spice now?

'Bit daring, even for you.' Gloria looks at Sandra's newly dyed red hair.

'How is he?' Sandra asks, stepping into the living room.

Gloria folds her arms. 'To be quite honest, Sandra, there was a bit of a 'to-do'.

Freddie is in a grey round neck t-shirt under a black blazer. 'So how did he get on with the aliens?' he says, playfully and whistles the theme tune from the *X-Files*.

'How do *you* know about our Jamie and all that UFO nonsense?' Gloria presses the anger into her pelvis somewhere. This, she has learnt over the last year. Letting it out in public never gets her anywhere, except in the supermarket where the staff all run for cover. It'll probably give her a tumour one day.

'He's been reading it. That book everyone is talking about,' Sandra says, inching slightly closer to Freddie. 'What's it called—*The Prophetic Insights*?'

'I don't think he is.' Gloria laughs, anger now leaking out of the seams. 'Our Jamie grew out of that rubbish a while ago.'

'Nah. I expect that's why he went to Taos,' Freddie says. 'That author, Prunella Small—she lives there. Says it in her biog.'

Gloria feels red mist rising around her. 'That *book*?' She's unable to find other words. Sandra and Freddie are both looking at her now, as if she's mentally ill. 'Well it had better not be in *this* house,' she says, eventually and heads to the door. 'Jamie, get down these stairs *now*.' She spits the words, the way she had when he was ten years old and had failed to tidy up after himself.

Roy walks in from the garage, a puzzled look on his face. 'What's going on?'

'Just keep out of this, Roy.' The palm of her hand comes up. 'This is between me and him.' Jamie's face appears at the door. 'Where is it?' she says. 'Don't pretend! You know exactly what I'm talking about. That book.'

Sandra touches Freddie on the shoulder. 'Perhaps we ought to just go.'

Roy says, 'Is this entirely necessary, Glo?'

Jamie leans against the doorframe, just as he had when he had been a boy in his pyjamas, upset that he'd been told to go to bed early. 'I-put-it-on-the-bookcase,' he says.

'Oh—I—could—bloody—swing—for—you!' She flies up the stairs. Even from the spare bedroom she can hear them talking about her.

'She's off,' Roy says. 'I knew it was a mistake to reduce her medication.'

On her knees, she reaches the bottom shelf, and finds it. 'I knew it.' Flicking through the pages, she notes, that it's been signed by the author. 'The divine truth will set you free,' she reads out loud, standing again, almost wrenching the door from its hinges and flying back into the living room.

Jamie is backed up against the bay window, nervously hugging a tasselled cushion cover. Roy asks again, 'What's going on?'

'*This* is what's going on,' Gloria confronts Jamie with a look of disgust. 'You know, I always granted you half a brain. But now I see that you don't even use that.' She raises the book at him like a weapon. 'Do you know how *worried* you've had us?'

Jamie holds out the palms of his hands in a gesture of apology. 'Mum, I didn't—'

'*He* got you reading this, didn't he?' she says. 'That Matthew. Oh, if I saw him now, I couldn't be held responsible—'

'I read it before I met him. Though he *had* read it. That's why we connected.'

Sandra reaches out for Gloria. 'Don't you think you should just calm down?'

'Connected?' The pitch of her voice is rising now, outside her own control. 'Like you had some sort of special bond over a fucking book.'

'Gloria!' Roy snaps, his face a little purple now.

'Well, *he's pushed* me to it. He'd make a saint swear,' she waves the book in the air. 'Everyone in the country has read it. But that doesn't mean it's any good.'

'How would *you* know?' Jamie says, flushed with embarrassment.

She shouldn't be doing this in front of them all. It's humiliating for him but she can't keep it in.

'I *know*,' she says, feeling she has the upper hand now, 'because

I've *read* it.'

Jamie gasps. 'You're lying! You'd never read a book like that.'

'You think you know everything,' Gloria says, spitefully. 'You're not the only one who reads. What did you think you'd find in there?' She starts tearing pages.

'No, Mum! Please!' Jamie rushes towards her, grasping for it.

Sandra shifts uncomfortably on the sofa. 'Maybe I should make the tea. Who'd like a nice cup of—'

Gloria pushes Jamie with a fist wrapped around a clump of torn paper. 'Get away from me,' she snarls, lips stretched across clenched teeth. 'Or I'll be sorry for what I do.'

'Mum, that's mine. Please—'

'Look what a bloody mess you got yourself into—moving in with that freak. I'm getting rid of this rubbish.' She tears more pages and throws them at Roy. 'This is because of you, this is.'

'Don't you start on me,' Roy says.

'*I* wanted to bring him back, that day. But it was you who said it was okay to leave him there, in that dump. That *squat*. With that cretin—the bloody Pied Piper of the self-help universe.'

'Good God!' Roy says, at last. 'I work all day and have to come home to *this*?'

Gloria looks at the ruined book in her hands. *Just breathe*, she thinks. She coolly passes the book to Roy, grasps a bit of dignity and wipes away angry tears.

'I only wanted some answers,' Jamie says.

Gloria looks at him now with incredulity. 'You know, some mothers take their kids to church, or mosque, or whatever. We didn't. We thought it'd be better you make up your own mind. I'd have saved up to send you on a Buddhist retreat rather than this. How could you let yourself get so taken in—to travel half-way across the world. Good God, I spent hundreds putting you through college. You're meant to be educated.'

'It wasn't meant to be like this,' Jamie says.

She looks around the room—the armchairs and sofa of her three-piece suite all pointing at the wide screen television that she and Roy sit in front of every weekend, hoping they might win the national lottery while the dust settled on her memories.

'Is this about the trip to America?' Roy says.

'Oh, the penny drops!' Gloria says.

'What was it? Was it some cult?' Roy asks.

'For want of a better word! He was in the middle of it! Our son, the *Pilgrim*. *You* saw that programme the other night. I told you at the time what he was getting mixed up with, but you wouldn't listen.'

Roy looks at the savaged book in his hands. 'What's the bloody book about?'

Gloria's hands go to her sides. 'Oh, it's just a load of old New-Age bullshit about how the universe is made up of energy and how we've come to evolve, you know, from energy to hydrogen atoms, from atoms and molecules and then into us.'

'Sounds pretty scientific,' Freddie says, smirking.

'When I want your opinion, Freddie, I'll ask for it.'

Sandra sits forward now. 'I don't think there's any need for—'

'The problem with it is,' Gloria continues, 'it suggests that we can harbour this energy in some way, leading to the next form of evolution, to learn to acquire psychic energy, thus connecting us to the universe.'

'Ah—I see,' Roy says, clearly non-the-wiser.

'And it's written by this woman who claims to have been *channelling* all these lessons from extraterrestrials on the other side of the universe—relatives of whom claim to have been re-born on Earth as lizards. Little green men. You've heard all that nonsense. And our Jamie po-goed across the world to become one of their students.'

'I went to see Matthew,' Jamie says. 'When I got there, he'd changed.' Tears roll down his face.

'It beats me how people fall for the stuff. It's just so trite. People have been listening to them for centuries—you know, the *voices*.' She's still snarling at Jamie. 'That's what *you* used to call *art* or *poetry*. And all of sudden, some freak comes along and calls it *channelling*. That Matthew has been wading around in a pool so shallow no ideas can actually live in it.' She sighs now. 'If you'd actually spent as much time writing a book as you have pondering the meaning of life, you'd have your first novel published.'

'Oh, Mum, I was so frightened.' Jamie begins to sob.

Gloria relents, taking him into her arms. 'Come, on love. That's it, let it out.'

'They said they were going to change me… they said…'

'I know love. They were just trying to frighten you.'

'Mum, I'm sorry. I really am. I didn't mean to worry you.'

Over Jamie's shoulder, Gloria can see Freddie fooling around. He's pulled up his blazer over his head so his face is surrounded by a cowl, arms retracted inside shortened sleeves. He sticks out the forefinger of his right hand, like the alien in Spielberg's movie and mimics a croaky voice, 'Phone home.'

Gloria lets go of Jamie, leans forward and in one uncompromised motion, she hits Freddie across the head, so hard it nearly spins.

'My God!' Sandra says.

'Gloria!' Roy says. 'You need to be sectioned, you do.'

Gloria rubs her face and teases her hair. Then for the first time since it had arrived, she pulls out the little glossy catalogue for Nebular Cruises that she'd discreetly hidden in the magazine rack. 'Look at this, Roy.'

'What's this?' he says.

'That's a ship. It's called *Miracle of the Universe*, would you believe.'

Roy flicks through the booklet. 'Look at these bloody prices.'

'Yes, I know. Sometimes life is expensive, Roy. I've decided I don't want to be stuck around here anymore. I want to swim in the sea. If there's one thing our Jamie has taught me, feeling secure isn't holding onto the edge. Security is swimming out into the middle, knowing you won't sink.'

Acknowledgements

A version of *Kissing the Lizard* was published within my larger collection of 'working-class' stories, *He's Done Ever So Well for Himself.*

This standalone version is a prequel to my novella, *The Pharmacist.* Thank you to the following for their invaluable feedback while readying this book for publication: Nathan Evans, Kit de Waal, Alex Hopkins, James Maker, Joshua Davies, Bartholomew Bennett and Jake Jones.

Thanks to all the Matthews in the world who tried my patience, and to Mum and Dad for keeping my feet on the ground.

Thanks as ever to Uli, Jimmy and Erica at the very splendid Gay's the Word Bookshop.

Thanks to our digital marketing guru, Sam Missingham.

Very special thanks to Benedicta Norell for her generous patronage which has helped to bring this book into being. And to Anthony Psaila, whose generous philanthropic efforts enabled me to get back to the desk and write again.

Lastly, thanks to everyone who keeps buying and reading the books. My loyal following—I love you.

Also from Inkandescent

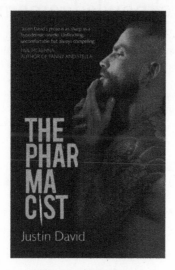

THE PHARMACIST
by Justin David

Twenty-four-year-old Billy is beautiful and sexy. Albert – The Pharmacist – is a compelling but damaged older man, and a veteran of London's late '90s club scene. After a chance meeting in the heart of the London's East End, Billy is seduced into the sphere of Albert. An unconventional friendship develops, fuelled by Albert's queer narratives and an endless supply of narcotics. Alive with the twilight times between day and night, consciousness and unconsciousness, the foundations of Billy's life begin to irrevocably shift and crack, as he fast-tracks toward manhood. This story of lust, love and loss is homoerotic bildungsroman at its finest.

'At the heart of David's *The Pharmacist* is an oddly touching and bizarre love story, a modern day *Harold and Maude* set in the drugged-up world of pre-gentrification Shoreditch. The dialogue, especially, bristles with glorious life.'
JONATHAN KEMP

'As lubricious as early Alan Hollinghurst, *The Pharmacist* is a welcome reissue from Inkandescent, and the perfect introduction to a singular voice in gay literature.'
THE TIMES LITERARY SUPPLEMENT

Also from Inkandescent

THE PALE ONES
by Bartholomew Bennett

Few books ever become loved. Most linger on undead, their sallow pages labyrinths of old, brittle stories and screeds of forgotten knowledge... And other things, besides: Paper-pale forms that rustle softly through their leaves. Ink-dark shapes swarming in shadow beneath faded type. And an invitation...

Harris delights in collecting the unloved. He wonders if you'd care to donate. A small something for the odd, pale children no-one has seen. An old book, perchance? Neat is sweet; battered is better. Broken spine or torn binding, stained or scarred - ugly doesn't matter. Not a jot. And if you've left a little of yourself between the pages – a receipt or ticket, a mislaid letter, a scrawled note or number – that's just perfect. He might call on you again.

Hangover Square meets *Naked Lunch* through the lens of a classic M. R. James ghost story. To hell and back again (and again) through Whitby, Scarborough and the Yorkshire Moors. Enjoy your Mobius-trip.

'A real addition to the literature of the uncanny and an impressive debut for its uncompromising author.'
RAMSEY CAMPBELL

Also from Inkandescent

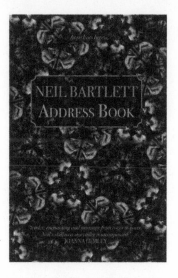

ADDRESS BOOK
by Neil Bartlett

Within the pages of this address book you will find not only names and places, but lives—with their everyday griefs and joys, and their everyday braveries.

A doctor revisits a formative sexual experience as he relocates in the midst of the coronavirus pandemic. A dancing queen takes ownership of his life—and first flat—at the height of the AIDS epidemic. A photographer develops a defiant passion in a Victorian tenement. A civil partnership celebration lowers barriers in a high-rise housing development. A priest comes up against the Home Office. In the Sixties, an expectant mother comes to accept a queer neighbour. Fifty years later, a widower comes to terms with the loss of a life partner.

Seven different times. Seven different situations. Seven different characters, each seeking to feel at home—somewhere or with someone. Let Bartlett lead you surefootedly between lives and locations, through decades of change to find hope in the strangest of places.

'Neil Bartlett is an all-seeing wizard'—EDMUND WHITE

Also from Inkandescent

MAINSTREAM
edited by Justin David & Nathan Evans

'A wonderful collection of fascinating stories by unique voices'
KATHY BURKE

This collection brings thirty authors in from the mar-gins to occupy centre-page. Queer storytellers. Working class wordsmiths. Chroniclers of colour. Writers whose life experiences give unique perspectives on universal challenges, whose voices must be heard. And read. Emerging writers are being placed alongside these established authors:

Bidisha, Elizabeth Baines, Gaylene Gould, Golnoosh Nour, Jonathan Kemp, Julia Bell, Keith Jarrett, Kerry Hudson, Kit de Waal, Juliet Jacques, Neil Bartlett, Neil McKenna, Padrika Tarrant, Paul McVeigh and Philip Ridley

'A riveting collection of stories, deftly articulated. Every voice entirely captivating: page to page, tale to tale. These are stories told with real heart from writers emerging from the margins in style.'
ASHLEY HICKSON-LOVENCE
author of *The 392* and *Your Show*

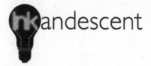**nkandescent**

Inkandescent Publishing was created in 2016
by Justin David and Nathan Evans to shine a light on
diverse and distinctive voices.

Sign up to our mailing list to stay informed
about future releases:

www.inkandescent.co.uk

by outsiders for outsiders

follow us on Facebook:

@InkandescentPublishing

and on Twitter:

@InkandescentUK